THE BARTLETT MYSTERY

LECTOR HOUSE PUBLIC DOMAIN WORKS

This book is a result of an effort made by Lector House towards making a contribution to the preservation and repair of original classic literature. The original text is in the public domain in the United States of America, and possibly other countries depending upon their specific copyright laws.

In an attempt to preserve, improve and recreate the original content, certain conventional norms with regard to typographical mistakes, hyphenations, punctuations and/or other related subject matters, have been corrected upon our consideration. However, few such imperfections might not have been rectified as they were inherited and preserved from the original content to maintain the authenticity and construct, relevant to the work. We believe that this work holds historical, cultural and/or intellectual importance in the literary works community, therefore despite the oddities, we accounted the work for print as a part of our continuing effort towards preservation of literary work and our contribution towards the development of the society as a whole, driven by our beliefs.

We are grateful to our readers for putting their faith in us and accepting our imperfections with regard to preservation of the historical content. We shall strive hard to meet up to the expectations to improve further to provide an enriching reading experience.

Though, we conduct extensive research in ascertaining the status of copyright before redeveloping a version of the content, in rare cases, a classic work might be incorrectly marked as not-in-copyright. In such cases, if you are the copyright holder, then kindly contact us or write to us, and we shall get back to you with an immediate course of action.

HAPPY READING!

THE BARTLETT MYSTERY

LOUIS TRACY

ISBN: 978-93-5344-109-8

First Published: -

© LECTOR HOUSE LLP

LECTOR HOUSE LLP
E-MAIL: lectorpublishing@gmail.com

THE BARTLETT MYSTERY

BY

LOUIS TRACY

Author of
"The Wings of the Morning," "Number Seventeen,"
etc., etc.

CONTENTS

Chapter *Page*

    I. A GATHERING AT A CLUB 1
   II. A DARING CRIME 6
  III. WINIFRED BARTLETT HEARS SOMETHING 12
  IV. FURTHER SURPRISES 19
   V. PERSECUTORS 26
  VI. BROTHER RALPH. 32
 VII. STILL MERE MYSTERY 39
VIII. THE DREAM FACE 44
  IX. THE FLIGHT. 49
   X. CARSHAW TAKES UP THE CHASE 56
  XI. THE TWO CARS. 62
 XII. THE PURSUIT 68
XIII. THE NEW LINK. 73
XIV. A SUBTLE ATTACK. 79
 XV. THE VISITOR 84
XVI. WINIFRED DRIFTS 88
XVII. ALL ROADS LEAD TO EAST ORANGE 93
XVIII. THE CRASH 98
XIX. CLANCY EXPLAINS 104
 XX. IN THE TOILS 109

CONTENTS

XXI. MOTHER AND SON 114
XXII. THE HUNT. 119
XXIII. "HE WHO FIGHTS AND RUNS AWAY—" 125
XXIV. IN FULL CRY 131
XXV. FLANK ATTACKS. 136
XXVI. THE BITER BIT 142
XXVII. THE SETTLEMENT 147

THE BARTLETT MYSTERY

CHAPTER I
A GATHERING AT A CLUB

That story of love and crime which figures in the records of the New York Detective Bureau as "The Yacht Mystery" has little to do with yachts and is no longer a mystery. It is concerned far more intimately with the troubles and trials of pretty Winifred Bartlett than with the vagaries of the restless sea; the alert, well-groomed figure of Winifred's true lover, Rex Carshaw, fills its pages to the almost total exclusion of the portly millionaire who owned the *Sans Souci*. Yet, such is the singular dominance exercised by the trivial things of life over the truly important ones, some hundreds of thousands of people in the great city on the three rivers will recall many episodes of the nine days' wonder known to them as "The Yacht Mystery" though they may never have heard of either Winifred or Rex.

It began simply, as all major events do begin, and, of course, at the outset, neither of these two young people seemed to have the remotest connection with it.

On the evening of October 5, 1913—that is the date when the first entry appears in the diary of Mr. James Steingall, chief of the Bureau—the stream of traffic in Fifth Avenue was interrupted to an unusual degree at a corner near Forty-second Street. The homeward-bound throng going up-town and the equally dense crowd coming down-town to restaurants and theater-land merely chafed at a delay which they did not understand, but the traffic policeman knew exactly what was going on, and kept his head and his temper.

A few doors down the north side of the cross street a famous club was ablaze with lights. Especially did three great windows on the first floor send forth hospitable beams, for the spacious room within was the scene of an amusing revel. Mr. William Pierpont Van Hofen, ex-commodore of the New York Yacht Club, owner of the *Sans Souci*, and multi-millionaire, had just astonished his friends by one of the eccentric jests for which he was famous.

The *Sans Souci*, notable the world over for its size, speed, and fittings, was going out of commission for the winter. Van Hofen had marked the occasion by widespread invitations to a dinner at his club, "to be followed by a surprise party," and the nature of the "surprise" was becoming known. Each lady had drawn by lot the name of her dinner partner, and each couple was then presented with a sealed envelope containing tickets for one or other of the many theaters in New York. Thus, not only were husbands, wives, eligible bachelors, and smart débutantes inextricably mixed up, but none knew whither the oddly assorted pairs were bound, since the envelopes were not to be opened until the meal reached the coffee and cigarette stage.

There existed, too, a secret within a secret. Seven men were bidden privately to come on board the *Sans Souci,* moored in the Hudson off the Eighty-sixth Street landing-stage, and there enjoy a quiet session of auction bridge.

"We'll duck before the trouble gets fairly started," explained Van Hofen to his cronies. "You'll see how the bunch is sorted out at dinner, but the tangle then will be just one cent in the dollar to the pandemonium when they find out where they're going."

Of course, everybody was acquainted with everybody else, or the joke might have been in bad taste. Moreover, as the gathering was confined exclusively to the elect of New York society, the host had notified the Detective Bureau, and requested the presence of one of their best men outside the club shortly before eight o'clock. None realized better than he that where the carcass is there the vultures gather, and he wanted no untoward incident to happen during the confusion which must attend the departure of so many richly bejeweled ladies accompanied by unexpected cavaliers.

Thus it befell that Detective-Inspector Clancy was detailed for the job. Steingall and he were the "inseparables" of the Bureau, yet no two members of a marvelously efficient service were more unlike, physically and mentally. Steingall was big, blond, muscular, a genial giant whose qualities rendered him almost popular among the very criminals he hunted, whereas those same desperadoes feared the diminutive Clancy, the little, slight, dark-haired sleuth of French-Irish descent. He, they were aware instinctively, read their very souls before Steingall's huge paw clutched their quaking bodies.

Idle chance alone decided that Clancy should undertake the half-hour's vigil at the up-town club that evening. All unknowing, he became thereby the controlling influence in many lives.

At eight o'clock an elderly man emerged from the building and edged his way through the cheery, laughing people already grouped about the doorway and awaiting automobiles. Mr. William Meiklejohn might have been branded with the word "Senator," so typical was he of the upper house at Washington. The very cut of his clothes, the style of his shoes, the glossiness of his hat, even the wide expanse of pearl-studded white linen marked him as a person of consequence.

A uniformed policeman, striving to keep the pavement clear of loiterers, recognized and saluted him. The salute was returned, though its recipient's face seemed to be gloomy, preoccupied, almost disturbed. Therefore he did not notice a gaunt, angular-jawed woman—one whose carriage and attire suggested better days long since passed—who had been peering eagerly at the revellers pouring out of the club, and now stepped forward impetuously as if to intercept him.

She failed. The policeman barred her progress quietly but effectually, and the woman, if bent on achieving her purpose, must have either called after the absorbed Meiklejohn or entered into a heated altercation with the policeman when accident came to her aid.

Mrs. Ronald Tower, strikingly handsome, richly gowned and cloaked, with an elaborate coiffure that outvied nature's best efforts, was crossing the pavement to enter a waiting car when she stopped and drew her hand from her escort's arm.

"Senator Meiklejohn!" she cried.

The elderly man halted. He doffed his hat with a flourish.

"Ah, Helen," he said smilingly. "Whither bound?"

"To see Belasco's latest. Isn't that lucky? The very thing I wanted. Poor Ronald! I don't know what has become of him, or into what net he may have fallen."

The Senator beamed. He knew that Ronald Tower was one of the eight bridge-players, but was pledged to secrecy.

"I only hailed you to jog your memory about that luncheon to-morrow," went on Mrs. Tower.

"How could I forget?" he retorted gallantly. "Only two hours ago I postponed a business appointment on account of it."

"So good of you, Senator," and Mrs. Tower's smile lent a tinge of sarcasm to the words. "I'm awfully anxious that you should meet Mr. Jacob. I'm deeply interested, you know."

Meiklejohn glanced rather sharply at the lady's companion, who, however, was merely a vacuous man about town. It struck Clancy that the Senator resented this incautious using of names. The shabby-genteel woman, hovering behind the policeman, was following the scene with hawklike eyes, and Clancy kept her, too, under close observation.

The Senator coughed, and lowered his voice.

"I shall be most pleased to discuss matters with him," he said. "It will be a pleasure to render him a service if you ask it."

Mrs. Tower laughed lightly. "One o'clock," she said. "Don't be late! Come along, Mr. Forrest. Your car is blocking the way."

Mr. Meiklejohn flourished his hat again. He turned and found himself face to face with the hard-featured woman who had been waiting and watching for this very opportunity. She barred his further progress—even caught his arm.

Had the Senator been assaulted by the blue-coated guardian of law and order he could not have displayed more bewilderment.

"You, Rachel?" he gasped.

The policeman was about to intervene, but it was the Senator, not the shabbily dressed woman, who prevented him.

"It's all right, officer," he stammered vexedly. "I know this lady. She is an old friend."

The man saluted again and drew aside. Clancy moved a trifle nearer. No one would take notice of such an insignificant little man. Though he had his back to this strangely assorted pair, he heard nearly every syllable they uttered.

"He is here," snapped the woman without other preamble. "You must see him."

"It is quite impossible," was the answer, and, though the words were frigid and unyielding, Clancy felt certain that Senator Meiklejohn had to exercise an iron self-control to keep a tremor out of his utterance.

"You dare not refuse," persisted the woman.

The Senator glanced around in a scared way. Clancy thought for an instant that he meant to dart back into the security of the club. After an irresolute pause, however, he moved somewhat apart from the crowd of sightseers. The two stood together on the curb, and clear of the flood of light pouring through the open doors. Clancy edged after them. He gathered a good deal, not all, of what they said, as both voices were harsh and tinged with excitement.

"This very night," the woman was saying. "Bring at least five hundred dollars—If the police.... Says he will confess everything.... Do you get me? This thing can't wait."

The Senator did not even try now to conceal his agitation. He looked at the gaping mob, but it was wholly absorbed in the stream of fashionable people pouring out of the club, while the snorting of scores of automobiles created a din which meant comparative safety.

"Yes, yes," he muttered. "I understand. I'll do anything in reason. I'll give *you* the money, and you——"

"No. He means seeing you. You need not be afraid. He says you are going to Mr. Van Hofen's yacht at nine o'clock——"

"Good Lord!" broke in Meiklejohn, "how can he possibly know that?" Again he peered at the press of onlookers. A dapper little man who stood near was raised on tiptoe and craning his neck to catch a glimpse of a noted beauty who had just appeared.

"Oh, pull yourself together!" and there was a touch of scorn in the woman's manner as she reassured this powerfully built man. "Isn't he clever and fertile in device? Haven't the newspapers announced your presence on the *Sans Souci*? And who will stop a steward's tongue from wagging? At any rate, he knows. He will be on the Hudson in a small boat, with one other man. At nine o'clock he will come close to the landing-stage at Eighty-sixth Street. There is a lawn north of the clubhouse, he says. Walk to the end of it and you will find him. You can have a brief talk. Bring the money in an envelope."

"On the lawn—at nine!" repeated the Senator in a dazed way.

"Yes. What better place could he choose? You see, he is willing to play fair and be discreet. But, quick! I must have your answer. Time is passing. Do you agree?"

A GATHERING AT A CLUB

"What is the alternative?"

"Capture, and a mad rage. Then others will share in his downfall."

"Very well. I'll be there. I'll not fail him, or you."

"He says it's his last request. He has some scheme——"

"Ah, his schemes! If only I could hope that this will be the end!"

"That is his promise."

The woman dropped the conversation abruptly. She darted through the line of cars and made off in the direction of Sixth Avenue. Senator Meiklejohn gazed after her dubiously, but her tall figure was soon lost in the traffic. Then, with bent head, and evidently a prey to harassing thoughts, he crossed Fifth Avenue.

Clancy sauntered after him, and saw him enter a block of residential flats in a side street. Then the detective strolled back to the club.

Most of Van Hofen's guests had gone. The policeman grinned and muttered in Clancy's ear:

"The Senator's a giddy guy. Two of 'em at wanst. Mrs. Tower's a good-looker, but I didn't think much of the other wan."

Clancy nodded. His black and beady eyes had just clashed with those of a notorious crook, who suddenly remembered an urgent appointment elsewhere.

Fifteen minutes later Senator Meiklejohn returned. He entered the club without being waylaid a second time. Clancy consulted his watch.

"Keep a sharp lookout here, Mac," he said, *sotto voce*. "While I was away just now Broadway Jim showed up. He's got cold feet, and there'll be nothing more doing to-night, I think. Anyhow, I'm going up-town."

In Fifth Avenue he boarded a Riverside Drive bus. The weather was mild, and he mounted to the roof.

"Now, who in the world will Senator Meiklejohn meet on the landing-stage?" he mused. "Seems to me the chief may be interested. Five hundred dollars, too! I wonder!"

CHAPTER II
A DARING CRIME

It was no part of Detective Clancy's business to pry into the private affairs of Senator Meiklejohn. Senators are awkward fish to handle, being somewhat similar to whales caught in nets designed to capture mackerel. But the Bureau is no respecter of persons. Men much higher up in politics and finance than William Meiklejohn would be disagreeably surprised if they could read certain details entered opposite their names in the *dossiers* kept by the police department. Still, it behooved Clancy to tread warily.

As it happened, he was just the man for this self-imposed duty. Two Celtic strains mingled in his blood, while American birth and training had not only quickened his intelligence but imparted a quality of wide-eyed shrewdness to a daring initiative. When he and the bluff Steingall worked together the malefactor on whose heels they pressed had a woeful time. As one blood-stained rascal put it in a bitter moment before the electric chair claimed him for the expiation of his last and worst crime:

"Them two guys give a reg'lar fellow no chanst. When they're trailin' you every road leads straight to Sing Sing. The big guy has a punch like Jess Willard, an' the lil 'un a nose like a Montana wolf."

It was Clancy's nose for the more subtle elements in crime which brought him to the small châlet on the private pier at the foot of Eighty-sixth Street that night. He could not guess what game he might flush, but he was keen as a bloodhound in the chase.

Meanwhile, Senator Meiklejohn encountered Ronald Tower the moment he re-entered the palatial club. By this time he seemed to have regained his customary air of geniality, being one of those rather uncommon men whose apparent characteristics are never so marked as when they are acting a part.

"H'lo, Ronnie," he cried affably, "I met Helen as she left for the theater. She has an inquiring mind, but I headed her off. By the way, will you be at this luncheon to-morrow?"

"Not I," laughed Tower. "I'm barred. She says I have no head for business, and some deep-laid plan for filling the family coffers is in hand."

The Senator obviously disliked these outspoken references to money-making.

He squirmed, but smiled as though Tower had made an excellent joke.

"Try and get the ukase lifted," he urged. "I want you to be there."

"Nothing doing," and the other grinned. "Helen says I resemble you in everything but brain power, Senator. I'm a good-looker as a husband, but a poor mutt in Wall Street."

They laughed at the conceit. The two men were curiously alike in face and figure, though a close observer like Clancy would have classed them as opposite as the poles in character and temperament. Meiklejohn's features were cast in the stronger mold. They showed lines which Ronald Tower's placid existence would never produce. The Senator was suave, too. He seldom pressed a point to the limit.

"Helen's good opinion is doubly flattering," he said. "She is a bright woman, and knows how to command her friends."

Tower glanced at a clock in the hall.

"Time we were off," he announced. "Come with me. I'm taking Johnny Bell, I think."

"Sorry. I have an important letter to write. But I'll join before the crowd cuts in."

The Senator hurried up-stairs. He must take the journey alone, and snatch an opportunity to attend that mysterious rendezvous while the *Sans Souci's* gig was ferrying some of the bridge-players to the yacht.

Owing to a slight misunderstanding Tower missed the other man, and traveled alone in his car. On that trivial circumstance hinged events which not only affected many lives but disturbed New York society more than any other incident within a decade.

Few among the thousands of summer promenaders who enjoy the magnificent panorama of the North River from the wooded heights of the Drive know of the pier at Eighty-sixth Street. For one thing, the clubhouse itself is an unpretentious structure; for another, the narrow and winding stairway leading down the side of the cliff gives no indication of its specific purpose. Moreover, a light footbridge across the tracks is hardly noticeable through the screen of trees and shrubs above, and the water-front lies yet fifty yards farther on.

At night the approach is not well lighted. In fact, no portion of the beautiful and precipitous riparian park is more secluded than the short stretch between the landing-stage and the busy thoroughfare on the crest.

That evening, as has been seen, Mr. Van Hofen was taking no risks for himself or his guests. A patrolman from the local precinct was stationed at the iron-barred gate on the landward end of the foot-bridge.

Clancy, on descending from the bus, stood for a few seconds and surveyed the scene. The night was dark and the sky overcast, but the myriad lights on the New Jersey shore were reflected in the swift current of the Hudson. The superb *Sans Souci* was easily distinguishable. All her ports were a-glow; lamps twinkled beneath the awnings on her after deck, and a boarding light indicated the lowered gangway.

The yacht was moored about three hundred feet from the landing-stage. Her graceful outlines were clearly discernible against the black, moving plain of the river. Just in that spot shone her radiance, lending a sense of opulence and security. For the rest, that part of New York's great waterway was dim and impalpable.

Try as he might, the detective could see no small craft afloat. The yacht's gig, waiting at the clubhouse, was hidden from view. He sped rapidly down the steps, and found the patrolman.

"That you, Nolan?" he said.

The man peered at him.

"Oh, Mr. Clancy, is it?" he replied.

"You know Senator Meiklejohn by sight?"

"Sure I do."

"When he comes along hail him. Say 'Good evening, Senator.' I'll hear you."

Clancy promptly moved off along the path which runs parallel with the railway. Nolan, though puzzled, put no questions, being well aware he would be told nothing more.

Three gentlemen came down the cliff, and crossed the bridge. One was Van Hofen himself. Now, the fates had willed that Ronald Tower should come next, and alone. He was hurrying. He had seen figures entering the club, and wanted to join them in the gig.

The policeman made the same mistake as many others.

"Good evenin', Senator," he said.

Tower nodded and laughed. He had no time to correct the harmless blunder. Even so, he was too late for the boat, which was already well away from the stage when he reached it. He lighted a cigarette, and strolled along the narrow terrace between river and lawn.

Clancy, on receiving his cue, followed Tower. An attendant challenged him at the iron gate, but Nolan certified that this diminutive stranger was "all right."

It was on the tip of the detective's tongue to ask if Mr. Meiklejohn had gone into the clubhouse when he saw, as he imagined, the Senator's tall form silhouetted against the vague carpet of the river; so he passed on, and this minor incident contributed its quota to a tragic occurrence. He heard some one behind him on the bridge, but paid no heed, his wits being bent on noting anything that took place in the semi-obscurity of the river's edge.

Meanwhile, the patrolman, encountering a double of Senator Meiklejohn, was dumbfounded momentarily. He sought enlightenment from the attendant.

"An', for the love of Mike, who was the first wan?" he demanded, when assured that the latest arrival was really the Senator.

"Mr. Ronald Tower," said the man. "They're like as two peas in a pod, ain't they?"

Nolan muttered something. He, too, crossed the bridge, meaning to find Clancy and explain his error. Thus, the four men were not widely separated, but Tower led by half a minute—long enough, in fact, to be at the north end of the terrace before Meiklejohn passed the gate.

There, greatly to his surprise, he looked down into a small motor-boat, with two occupants, keeping close to the sloping wall. The craft and its crew could have no reasonable business there. They suggested something sinister and furtive. The engine was stopped, and one of the men, huddled up in the bows, was holding the boat against the pull of the tide by using a boathook as a punting pole.

Tower, though good-natured and unsuspicious, was naturally puzzled by this apparition. He bent forward to examine it more definitely, and rested his hands on a low railing. Then he was seen by those below.

"That you?" growled the second man, standing up suddenly.

"It is," said Tower, speaking with strict accuracy, and marveling now who on earth could have arranged a meeting at such a place and in such bizarre conditions.

"Well, here I am," came the gruff announcement. "The cops are after me. Some one must have tipped them off. If it was you I'll get to know and even things up, P. D. Q. Chew on that during the night's festivities, I advise you. Brought that wad?"

Tower was the last man breathing to handle this queer situation discreetly. He ought to have temporized, but he loathed anything in the nature of vulgar or criminal intrigue. Being quick-tempered withal, if deliberately insulted, he resented this fellow's crude speech.

"No," he cried hotly. "What you really want is a policeman, and there's one close at hand—Hi! Officer!" he shouted: "Come here at once. There are two rascals in a boat—"

Something swirled through the darkness, and his next word was choked in a cry of mortal fear, for a lasso had fallen on his shoulders and was drawn taut. Before he could as much as lift his hands he was dragged bodily over the railing and headlong into the river.

Clancy, forced by circumstances to remain at a distance, could only overhear Tower's share in the brief conversation. The tones in the voice perplexed him, but the preconcerted element in the affair seemed to offer proof positive that Senator Meiklejohn had kept his appointment. He was just in time to see Tower's legs disappearing, and a loud splash told what had happened. He was not armed. He never carried a revolver unless the quest of the hour threatened danger or called for a display of force. In a word, he was utterly powerless.

Senator Meiklejohn, alive to the vital fact that some one on the terrace had discovered the boat, hung back dismayed. He was joined by Nolan, who could not understand the sudden commotion.

"What's up?" Nolan asked. "Didn't some wan shout?"

Clancy, in all his experience of crime and criminals, had never before encountered such an amazing combination of unforeseen conditions. The boat's motor was already chugging breathlessly, and the small craft was curving out into the gloom. He saw a man hauling in a rope from the stern, and well did he know why the cord seemed to be attached to a heavy weight. Not far away he made out the yacht's gig returning to the stage.

"*Sans Souci* ahoy!" he almost screamed. "Head off that launch! There's murder done!"

It was a hopeless effort, of course, though the sailors obeyed instantly, and bent to their oars. Soon they, too, vanished in the murk, but, finding they were completely outpaced, came back seeking for instructions which could not be given. The detective thought he was bewitched when he ran into Senator Meiklejohn, pallid and trembling, standing on the terrace with Nolan.

"You?" he shrieked in a shrill falsetto. "Then, in heaven's name, who is the man who has just been pulled into the river?"

"Tower!" gasped the Senator. "Mr. Ronald Tower. They mistook him for me."

"Faith, an' I did that same," muttered the patrolman, whose slow-moving wits could assimilate only one thing at a time.

Clancy, afire with rage and a sense of inexplicable failure, realized that Meiklejohn's admission and its now compulsory explanation could wait a calmer moment. The club attendant, attracted by the hubbub, raced to the lawn, and the detective tackled him.

"Isn't there a motor launch on the yacht?" he asked.

"Yes, sir, but it'll be all sheeted up on deck."

"Have you a megaphone?"

"Yes."

The man ran and grabbed the instrument from its hook, so Clancy bellowed the alarming news to Mr. Van Hofen and the others already on board the *Sans Souci* that Ronald Tower had been dragged into the river and probably murdered. But what could they do? The speedy rescue of Tower, dead or alive, was simply impossible.

The gig arrived. Clancy stormed by telephone at a police station-house and at the up-river station of the harbor police, but such vain efforts were the mere necessities of officialdom. None knew better than he that an extraordinary crime had been carried through under his very eyes, yet its daring perpetrators had escaped, and he could supply no description of their appearance to the men who would watch the neighboring ferries and wharves.

Van Hofen and his friends, startled and grieved, came ashore in the gig, and Clancy was striving to give them some account of the tragedy without revealing its inner significance when his roving glance missed Meiklejohn from the distraught group of men.

"Where is the Senator?" he cried, turning on the gaping Nolan.

"Gee, he's knocked out," said the policeman. "He axed me to tell you he'd gone down-town. Ye see, some wan has to find Mrs. Tower."

Clancy's black eyes glittered with fury, yet he spoke no word. A blank silence fell on the rest. They had not thought of the bereaved wife, but Meiklejohn had remembered. That was kind of him. The Senator always did the right thing. And how he must be suffering! The Towers were his closest friends!

CHAPTER III.
WINIFRED BARTLETT HEARS SOMETHING

Early next morning a girl attired in a neat but inexpensive costume entered Central Park by the One Hundred and Second Street gate, and walked swiftly by a winding path to the exit on the west side at One Hundredth Street.

She moved with the easy swing of one to whom walking was a pleasure. Without hurry or apparent effort her even, rapid strides brought her along at a pace of fully four miles an hour. And an hour was exactly the time Winifred Bartlett needed if she would carry out her daily program, which, when conditions permitted, involved a four-mile detour by way of Riverside Drive and Seventy-second Street to the Ninth Avenue "L." This morning she had actually ten minutes in hand, and promised herself an added treat in making little pauses at her favorite view-points on the Hudson.

To gain this hour's freedom Winifred had to practise some harmless duplicity, as shall be seen. She was obliged to rise long before the rest of her fellow-workers in the bookbinding factory of Messrs. Brown, Son & Brown, an establishment located in the least inviting part of Greenwich Village.

But she went early to bed, and the beams of the morning sun drew her forth as a linnet from its nest. Unless the weather was absolutely prohibitive she took the walk every day, for she revelled in the ever-changing tints of the trees, the music of the songbirds, and the gambols of the squirrels in the park, while the broad highway of the river, leading to and from she hardly knew what enchanted lands, brought vague dreams of some delightful future where daily toil would not claim her and she might be as those other girls of the outer world to whom existence seemed such a joyous thing.

Winifred was not discontented with her lot—the ichor of youth and good health flowed too strongly in her veins. But at times she was bewildered by a sense of aloofness from the rest of humanity.

Above all did she suffer from the girls she met in the warehouse. Some were coarse, nearly every one was frivolous. Their talk, their thinly-veiled allusions to a night life in which she bore no part, puzzled and disturbed her. True, the wild revels of which they boasted did not sound either marvelous or attractive when analyzed. A couple of hours at the movies, a frolic in a dance hall, a quarrel about some youthful gallant, violent fluctuations from arm-laced friendship to sparkling-eyed hatred and back again to tears and kisses—these joys and cankers formed the limited gamut of their emotions.

For all that, Winifred could not help asking herself with ever increasing insistence why she alone, among a crude, noisy sisterhood of a hundred young women of her own age, should be with them yet not of them. She realized that her education fitted her for a higher place in the army of New York workers than a bookbinder's bench. She could soon have acquired proficiency as a stenographer. Pleasant, well-paid situations abounded in the stores and wholesale houses. There was even some alluring profession called "the stage," where a girl might actually earn a living by singing and dancing, and Winifred could certainly sing and was certain she could dance if taught.

What queer trick of fate, then, had brought her to Brown, Son & Brown's in the spring of that year, and kept her there? She could not tell. She could not even guess why she dwelt so far up-town, while every other girl in the establishment had a home either in or near Greenwich Village.

Heigho! Life was a riddle. Surely some day she would solve it.

Her mind ran on this problem more strongly than usual that morning. Still pondering it, she diverged for a moment at the Soldiers' and Sailors' Monument, and stood on the stone terrace which commands such a magnificent stretch of the silvery Hudson, with the green heights of the New Jersey shore directly opposite, and the Palisades rearing their lofty crests away to the north.

Suddenly she became aware that a small group of men had gathered there, and were displaying a lively interest in two motor boats on the river. Something out of the common had stirred them; voices were loud and gestures animated.

"Look!" said one, "they've gotten that boat!"

"You can't be sure," doubted another, though his manner showed that he wanted only to be convinced.

"D'ye think a police launch 'ud be foolin' around with a tow at this time o' day if it wasn't something special?" persisted the first speaker. "Can't yer see it's empty? There's a cop pointin' now to the clubhouse."

"Good for you," pronounced the doubtful one. The pointing cop had clinched the argument.

"An' they're headin' that way," came the cry.

Off raced the men. Winifred found that people on top of motor-omnibuses scurrying down-town were also watching the two craft. Opposite the end of Eighty-sixth Street such a crowd assembled as though by magic that she could not see over the railings. She could not imagine why people should be so worked up by the mere finding of an empty boat. She heard allusions to names, but they evoked no echo in her mind. At last, approaching a girl among the sightseers, she put a timid question:

"Can you tell me what is the matter?" she said.

"They've found the boat," came the ready answer.

"Yes, but what boat? Why any boat?"

"Haven't you read about the murder last night. Mr. Van Hofen, who owns that yacht there, the *San Sowsy*, had a party of friends on board, an' one of 'em was dragged into the river an' drowned. Nice goin's on. *San Sowsy*—it's a good name for the whole bunch, I guess."

Winifred did not understand why the girl laughed.

"What a terrible thing!" she said. "Perhaps it was only an accident; and sad enough at that if some poor man lost his life."

"Oh, no. It's a murder right enough. The papers are full of it. I was walkin' here at nine o'clock with a fellow. It might ha' been done under me very nose. What d'ye know about that?"

"It's very sad," repeated Winifred. "Such dreadful things seem to be almost impossible under this blue sky and in bright sunshine. Even the river does not look cruel."

She went on, having no time for further dawdling. Her informant glanced after her curiously, for Winifred's cheap clothing and worn shoes were oddly at variance with her voice and manner.

At Seventy-second Street Winifred bought a newspaper, which she read instead of the tiny volume of Browning's poems carried in her hand-bag. She always contrived to have a book or periodical for the train journeys, since men had a way of catching her eye when she glanced around thoughtlessly, and such incidents were annoying. She soon learned the main details of "The Yacht Mystery." The account of Ronald Tower's dramatic end was substantially accurate. It contained, of course, no allusion to Senator Meiklejohn's singular connection with the affair, but Clancy had taken care that a disturbing paragraph should appear with the rest of a lurid write-up.

"Sinister rumors are current in clubland," read Winifred. "These warrant the belief that others beside the thugs in the boat are implicated in the tragedy. Indeed, it is whispered that a man high in the political world can, if he chooses, throw light on what is, at this writing, an inexplicable crime, a crime which would be incredible if it had not actually taken place."

The reporter did not know, and Clancy did not tell him, just what this innuendo meant. The detective was anxious that Senator Meiklejohn should realize the folly of refusing all information to the authorities, and this thinly-veiled threat of publicity was one way of bringing him to his senses.

Winifred had never before come into touch, so to speak, with any deed of criminal violence. She was so absorbed in the story of the junketing at a fashionable club, with its astounding sequel in a locality familiar to her eyes, that she hardly noticed a delay on the line.

She did not even know that she would be ten minutes late until she saw a clock at Fourteenth Street. Then she raced to the door of a big, many-storied building.

A timekeeper shook his head at her, but, punctual as a rule, on wet mornings she was invariably the first to arrive, so the watch-dog compromised on the give-and-take principle. When she emerged from the elevator at the ninth floor her cheeks were still suffused with color, her eyes were alight, her lips parted under the spell of excitement and haste. In a word, she looked positively bewitching.

Two people evidently took this view of her as she advanced into the workroom after hanging up her hat and coat.

"You're late again, Bartlett," snapped Miss Agatha Sugg, a forewoman, whose initials suggested an obvious nickname among the set of flippant girls she ruled with a severity that was also ungracious. "I'll not speak to you any more on the matter. Next time you'll be fired. See?"

Winifred's high color fled before this dire threat. Even the few dollars a week she earned by binding books was essential to the up-keep of her home. At any rate this fact was dinned into her ears constantly, and formed a ready argument against any change of employment.

"I'm sorry, Miss Sugg," she stammered. "I didn't think I had lost any time. Indeed, I started out earlier than usual."

"Rubbish!" snorted Miss Sugg. "What're givin' me? It's a fine day."

"Yes," said Winifred timidly, "but unfortunately I stopped a while on Riverside Drive to watch the police bringing in the boat from which Mr. Tower was mur—pulled into the river last night."

"Riverside Drive!" snapped the forewoman. "Your address is East One Hundred and Twelfth Street, ain't it? What were you doing on Riverside Drive?"

"I walk that way every morning unless it is raining."

Miss Sugg looked incredulous, but felt that she was traveling outside her own territory.

"Anyhow," she said, "that's your affair, not mine, an' it's no excuse for bein' late."

"Oh, come now," intervened a man's voice, "this young lady is not so far behind time as to cause such a row. She can pull out a bit and make up for it."

Miss Sugg wheeled wrathfully to find Mr. Fowle, manager on that floor, gazing at Winifred with marked approval. Fowle, a shifty-eyed man of thirty, compactly built, and somewhat of a dandy, seldom gave heed to any of the girls employed by Brown, Son & Brown. His benevolent attitude toward Winifred was a new departure.

"Young lady!" gasped the forewoman. She was in such a temper that other words failed.

"Yes, she isn't an old one," smirked Fowle. "That's all right, Miss Bartlett, get on with your work. Miss Sugg's bark is worse than her bite."

Though he had poured oil on the troubled waters his air was not altogether reassuring. Winifred went to her bench in a flurry of trepidation. She dreaded the vixenish Miss Sugg less than the too complaisant manager. Somehow, she fancied that he would soon speak to her again; when, a few minutes later, he drew near, and she felt rather than saw that he was staring at her boldly, she flushed to the nape of her graceful neck.

Yet he put a quite orthodox question.

"Did I get your story right when you came in?" he said. "I think you told Miss Sugg that the harbor police had picked up the motor-boat in that yacht case."

"So I heard," said Winifred. She was in charge of a wire-stitching machine, and her deft fingers were busy. Moreover, she was resolved not to give Fowle any pretext for prolonging the conversation.

"Who told you?"

The manager's tone grew a trifle less cordial. He was not accustomed to being held at arm's length by any young woman in the establishment whom he condescended to notice.

"I really don't know," and Winifred began placing her array of work in sorted piles. "Indeed, I spoke carelessly. No one told me. I saw a commotion on Riverside Drive, and heard a man arguing with others that a boat then being towed by a police launch must be the missing one."

Fowle's whiff of annoyance had passed. He had jumped to the conclusion that such an extremely pretty girl would surely own a sweetheart who escorted her to and from work each day. He did not suspect that every junior clerk downstairs had in turn offered his services in this regard, but with such lack of success that each would-be suitor deemed Winifred conceited.

"I wish I had been there," he said. "Do you go home the same way?"

"No."

Winifred was aware that the other girls were watching her furtively and exchanging meaning looks.

"You take the Third Avenue L, I suppose?" persisted Fowle. Then Winifred faced him squarely. For some reason her temper got the better of her.

"It is a house rule, Mr. Fowle," she said, "that the girls are forbidden to talk during working hours."

"Nonsense," laughed Fowle. "I'm in charge here, an' what I say goes."

He left her, however, and busied himself elsewhere. Apparently, he was even forgiving enough to call Miss Sugg out of the room and detain her all the rest of the morning.

Winifred was promptly rallied by some of her companions.

"I must say this for you, Winnie Bartlett, you don't think you're the whole shootin' match," said a stout, red-faced creature, who would have been more at home on a farm than in a New York warehouse, "but it gets my goat when you hand the mustard to Fowle in that way. If he made goo-goo eyes at me, I'd play, too."

"I wish little Carlotta was a blue-eyed, golden-haired queen," sighed another, a squat Neapolitan with the complexion of a Moor. "She's give Fowle a chance to dig into his pocketbook, believe me."

The youthful philosopher won a chorus of approval. All the girls liked Winifred. They even tacitly admitted that she belonged to a different order, and seldom teased her. Fowle's obvious admiration, however, imposed too severe a strain, and their tongues ran freely.

The luncheon-hour came, and Winifred hurried out with the others. They patronized a restaurant in Fourteenth Street. At a news-stand she purchased an evening paper, a rare event, since she had to account for every cent of expenditure. Though allowed books, she was absolutely forbidden newspapers!

But this forlorn girl, who knew so little of the great city in whose life she was such an insignificant item, felt oddly concerned in "The Yacht Mystery." It was the first noteworthy event of which she had even a remote first-hand knowledge. That empty launch, its very abandonment suggesting eeriness and fatality, was a tangible thing. Was she not one of the few who had literally seen it? So she invested her penny, and after reading of the discovery of the boat—it was found moored to a wharf at the foot of Fort Lee—breathlessly read:

As the outcome of information given by a well-known Senator, the police have obtained an important clue which leads straight to a house in One Hundred and Twelfth Street.

"Well," mused Winifred, wide-eyed with astonishment. "Fancy that! The very street where I live!"

She read on:

The arrest of at least one person, a woman, suspected of complicity in the crime may occur at any moment. Detectives are convinced that the trail of the murderers will soon be clearer.

Every effort is being made to recover Mr. Tower's body, which, it is conceivable, may have been weighted and sunk in the river near the spot where the boat was tied.

Winifred gave more attention to the newspaper report than to her frugal meal. Resolving, however, that Miss Sugg should have no further cause for complaint that day, she returned to the factory five minutes before time. An automobile was standing outside the entrance, but she paid no heed to it.

The checker tapped at his little window as she passed.

"The boss wants you," he said.

"Me!" she cried. Her heart sank. Between Miss Sugg and Mr. Fowle she had already probably lost her situation!

"Yep," said the man. "You're Winifred Bartlett, I guess. Anyhow, if there's another peach like you in the bunch I haven't seen her."

She bit her lip and tears trembled in her eyes. Perhaps the gruff Cerberus behind the window sympathized with her. He lowered his voice to a hoarse whisper: "There's a cop in there, an' a 'tec,' too."

Winifred was startled out of her forebodings.

"They cannot want me!" she said amazedly.

"You never can tell, girlie. Queer jinks happen sometimes. I wouldn't bat an eyelid if they rounded up the boss hisself."

She was sure now that some stupid mistake had been made. At any rate, she no longer dreaded dismissal, and the first intuition of impending calamity yielded to a nervous curiosity as she pushed open a door leading to the general office.

CHAPTER IV
FURTHER SURPRISES

A clerk, one of the would-be swains who had met with chilling discouragement after working-hours, was evidently on the lookout for her. An ignoble soul prompted a smirk of triumph now.

"Go straight in," he said, jerking a thumb. "A cop's waitin' for you."

Winifred did not vouchsafe him even an indignant glance. Holding her head high, she passed through the main office, and made for a door marked "Manager." She knocked, and was admitted by Mr. Fowle. Grouped around a table she saw one of the members of the firm, the manager, a policeman, and a dapper little man, slight of figure, who held himself very erect. He was dressed in blue serge, and had the ivory-white face and wrinkled skin of an actor. She was conscious at once of the penetration of his glance. His eyes were black and luminous. They seemed to pierce her with an X-ray quality of comprehension.

"This is the girl," announced Mr. Fowle deferentially.

The little man in the blue suit took the lead forthwith.

"You are Winifred Bartlett?" he said, and by some subtle inter-flow of magnetism Winifred knew instantly that she had nothing to fear from this diminutive stranger.

"Yes," she replied, looking at him squarely.

"You live in East One Hundred and Twelfth Street?"

"Yes."

"With a woman described as your aunt, and known as Miss Rachel Craik?"

"Yes."

Each affirmative marked a musical crescendo. Especially was Winifred surprised by the sceptical description of her only recognized relative.

"Well," went on Clancy, suppressing a smile at the girl's naïve astonishment, "don't be alarmed, but I want you to come with me to Mulberry Street."

Now, Winifred had just been reading about certain activities in Mulberry Street, and her eyebrows rounded in real amazement.

"Isn't that the Police Headquarters?" she asked.

Fowle chuckled, whereupon Clancy said pleasantly:

"Yes. One man here seems to know the address quite intimately. But that fact need not set your heart fluttering. The chief of the Detective Bureau wishes to put a few questions. That is all."

"Questions about what?"

Winifred's natural dignity came to her aid. She refused to have this grave matter treated as a joke.

"Take my advice, Miss Bartlett, and don't discuss things further until you have met Mr. Steingall," said Clancy.

"But I have never even heard of Mr. Steingall," she protested. "What right have you or he to take me away from my work to a police-station? What wrong have I done to any one?"

"None, I believe."

"Surely I have a right to some explanation."

"If you insist I am bound to answer."

"Then I do insist," and Winifred's heightened color and wrathful eyes only enhanced her beauty. Clancy spread his hands in a gesture inherited from a French mother.

"Very well," he said. "You are required to give evidence concerning the death of Mr. Ronald Tower. Now, I cannot say any more. I have a car outside. You will be detained less than an hour. The same car will bring you back, and I think I can guarantee that your employers will raise no difficulty."

The head of the firm growled agreement. As a matter of fact the staid respectability of Brown, Son & Brown had sustained a shock by the mere presence of the police. Murder has an ugly aspect. It was often bound up in the firm's products, but never before had it entered that temple of efficiency in other guise.

Clancy sensed the slow fermentation of the pharisaical mind.

"If I had known what sort of girl this was I would never have brought a policeman," he muttered into the great man's ear. "She has no more to do with this affair than you have."

"It is very annoying—very," was the peevish reply.

"What is? Assisting the police?"

"Oh, no. Didn't mean that, of course."

The detective thought he might do more harm than good by pressing for a definition of the firm's annoyance. He turned to Winifred.

"Are you ready, Miss Bartlett?" he said. "The only reason the Bureau has for troubling you is the accident of your address."

Almost before the girl realized the new and astounding conditions which had

FURTHER SURPRISES 21

come into her life she was seated in a closed automobile and speeding swiftly down-town.

She was feminine enough, however, to ply Clancy with questions, and he had to fence with her, as it was all-important that such information as she might be able to give should be imparted when he and Steingall could observe her closely. The Bureau hugged no delusions. Its vast experience of the criminal world rendered misplaced sympathy with erring mortals almost impossible. Young or old, rich or poor, beautiful or ugly, the strange procession which passes in unending review before the police authorities is subjected to impartial yet searching analysis. Few of the guilty ones escape suspicion, no matter how slight the connecting clue or scanty the evidence. On the other hand, Steingall and his trusty aid seldom made a mistake when they decided, as Clancy had already done in Winifred's case, that real innocence had come under the shadow of crime.

Steingall shared Clancy's opinion the instant he set eyes on the new witness. He gazed at her with a humorous dismay that was wholly genuine.

"Sit there, Miss Bartlett," he said, rising to place a chair for her. "Please don't feel nervous. I am sure you understand that only those who have broken the law need fear it. Now, *you* haven't killed anybody, have you?"

Winifred smiled. She liked this big man's kindly manner. Really, the police were not such terrifying ogres when you came to close quarters with them.

"No, indeed," she said, little guessing that Clancy had indulged in a Japanese grimace behind her back, thereby informing his chief that "The Yacht Mystery" was still maintaining its claim to figure as one of the most sensational crimes the Bureau had investigated during many a year.

Steingall, wishing to put the girl wholly at ease, affected to consult some notes on his desk, but Winifred was too wrought up to keep silent.

"The gentleman who brought me here told me that I would be required to give evidence concerning the murder of Mr. Ronald Tower," she said. "Believe me, sir, that unfortunate gentleman's name was unknown to me before I read it in this morning's paper. I have no knowledge of the manner of his death other than is contained in the account printed here in this newspaper."

She proffered the newspaper purchased before lunch, which she still held in her left hand. The impulsive action broadened Steingall's smile. He was still utterly at a loss to account for this well-mannered girl's queer environment.

"Why," he cried, "I quite understand that. Mr. Clancy didn't tell you we regarded you as a desperate crook, did he?"

Winifred yielded to the chief's obvious desire to lift their talk out of the rut of formality. She could not help being interested in these two men, so dissimilar in their characteristics, yet each so utterly unlike the somewhat awesome personage she would have sketched if asked to define her idea of a "detective." Clancy, who had taken a chair at the side of the table, sat on it as though he were an automaton built of steel springs and ready to bounce instantly in any given direction. Steingall's huge bulk lolled back indolently. He had been smoking when the others entered, and a half-consumed cigar lay on an ash-tray. Winifred thought it would be rather amusing if she, in turn, made things comfortable.

"Please don't put away your cigar on my account," she said. "I like the smell of good tobacco."

"Ha!" cackled Clancy.

"Thank you," said Steingall, tucking the Havana into a corner of his mouth. The two men exchanged glances, and Winifred smiled. Steingall's look of tolerant contempt at his assistant was distinctly amusing.

"That little shrimp can't smoke, Miss Bartlett," he explained, "so he is an anti-tobacco maniac."

"You wouldn't care to take poison, would you?" and Clancy shot the words at Winifred so sharply that she was almost startled.

"No. Of course not," she agreed.

"Yet that is what that mountain of brawn does during fourteen hours out of the twenty-four. Nicotine is one of the deadliest poisons known to science. Even when absorbed into the tissues in minute doses it corrodes the brain and atrophies the intellect. Did you see how he grinned when you described that vile weed as 'good tobacco'? Now, you don't know good, meaning real, tobacco from bad, do you?"

"I know whether or not I like the scent of it," persisted Winifred. She began to think that officialdom in Mulberry Street affected the methods of the court circles frequented by Alice and the Mad Hatter.

"Don't mind him," put in Steingall genially. "He's a living example of the close alliance between insanity and genius. On the tobacco question he's simply cracked, and that is all there is to it. Now we're wasting your time by this chatter. I'll come to serious business by asking a question which you will not find embarrassing for a good many years yet to come. How old are you?"

"Nineteen last birthday."

"When were you born?"

"On June 6, 1894."

"And where?"

Winifred reddened slightly.

"I don't know," she said.

"What?"

Steingall seemed to be immensely surprised, and Winifred proceeded forthwith to throw light on this singular admission, which was exactly what he meant her to do.

"That is a very odd statement, but it is quite true," she said earnestly. "My aunt would never tell me where I was born. I believe it was somewhere in the New England States, but I have only the vaguest grounds for the opinion. What I mean is that aunty occasionally reveals a close familiarity with Boston and Vermont."

"What is her full name?"

"Rachel Craik."

"She has never been married?"

Winifred's sense of humor was keen. She laughed at the idea of "Aunt Rachel" having a husband.

"I don't think aunty will ever marry anybody now," she said. "She holds the opposite sex in detestation. No man is ever admitted to our house."

"It is a small, old-fashioned residence, but very large for the requirements of two women?" continued Steingall. He took no notes, and might have been discussing the weather, now that the first whiff of wonderment as to Winifred's lack of information about her birth-place had passed.

"Yes. We have several rooms unoccupied."

"And unfurnished?"

"Say partly furnished."

"Ever had any boarders?"

"No."

"No servants, of course?"

"No."

"And how long have you been employed in Messrs. Brown, Son & Brown's bookbinding department?"

"About six months."

"What do you earn?"

"Eight dollars a week."

"Is that the average amount paid to the other girls?"

"Slightly above the average. I am supposed to be quick and accurate."

"Well now, Miss Bartlett, you seem to be a very intelligent and well-educated young woman. How comes it that you are employed in such work?"

"It was the best I could find," she volunteered.

"No doubt. But you must be well aware that few, if any, among the girls in the bookbinding business can be your equal in education, and, may I add, in refinement. Now, if you were a bookkeeper, a cashier or a typist, I could understand it; but it does seem odd to me that you should be engaged in this kind of job."

"It was my aunt's wish," said Winifred simply.

"Ah!"

Steingall dwelt on the monosyllable.

"What reason did she give for such a singular choice?" he went on.

"I confess it has puzzled me," was the unaffected answer. "Although aunty is severe in her manner she is well educated, and she taught me nearly all I know, except music and singing, for which I took lessons from Signor Pecci ever since I was a tiny mite until about two years ago. Then, I believe, aunty lost a good deal of money, and it became necessary that I should earn something. Signor Pecci offered to get me a position in a theater, but she would not hear of it, nor would she allow me to enter a shop or a restaurant. Really, it was aunty who got me work with Messrs. Brown, Son & Brown."

"In other words," said Steingall, "you were deliberately reared to fill a higher social station, and then, for no assignable reason, save a whim, compelled to sink to a much lower level?"

"I do not know. I never disputed aunty's right to do what she thought best."

"Well, well, it is odd. Do you ever entertain any visitors?"

"None whatever. We have no acquaintances, and live very quietly."

"Do you mean to say that your aunt never sees any one but yourself and casual callers, such as tradespeople?"

"So far as I know, that is absolutely the case."

"Very curious," commented Steingall. "Does your aunt go out much?"

"She leaves the house occasionally after I have gone to bed at ten o'clock, but that is seldom, and I have no idea where she goes. Every week-day, you know, I am away from home between seven in the morning and half past six at night, excepting Saturday afternoons. If possible, I take a long walk before going to work."

"Do you go straight home?"

Winifred remembered Mr. Fowle's query, and smiled again.

"Yes," she said.

"Now last night, for instance, was your aunt at home when you reached the house?"

"No; she was out. She did not come in until half past nine."

"Did she go out again last night?"

"I do not know. I was tired. I went to bed rather early."

Steingall bent over his notes for the first time since Winifred appeared. His lips were pursed, and he seemed to be weighing certain facts gravely.

"I think," he said at last, "that I need not detain you any longer, Miss Bartlett. By the way, I'll give you a note to your employers to say that you are in no way connected with the crime we have under investigation. It may, perhaps, save you needless annoyance."

"Thank you, sir," said the girl. "But won't you tell me why you have asked me so many questions about my aunt and her ways?"

Steingall looked at her thoughtfully before he answered: "In the first place,

FURTHER SURPRISES 25

Miss Bartlett, tell me this. I assume Miss Craik is your mother's sister. When did your mother die?"

Winifred blushed with almost childish discomfiture. "It may seem very stupid to say such a thing," she admitted, "but I have never known either a father or a mother. My aunt has always refused to discuss our family affairs in any way whatever. I fear her view is that I am somewhat lucky to be alive at all."

"Few people would be found to agree with her," said the chief gallantly. "Now I want you to be brave and patient. A very extraordinary crime has been committed, and the police occasionally find clues in the most unexpected quarters. I regret to tell you that Miss Craik is believed to be in some way connected with the mysterious disappearance, if not the death, of Mr. Ronald Tower, and she is being held for further inquiries."

Winifred's face blanched. "Do you mean that she will be kept in prison?" she said, with a break in her voice.

"She must be detained for a while, but you need not be so alarmed. Her connection with this outrage may be as harmless as your own, though I can inform you that, without your knowledge, your house last night certainly sheltered two men under grave suspicion, and for whom we are now searching."

"Two men! In our house!" cried the amazed girl.

"Yes. I tell you this to show you the necessity there is for calmness and reticence on your part. Don't speak to any one concerning your visit here. Above all else, don't be afraid. Have you any one with whom you can go to live until Miss Craik is"—he corrected himself—"until matters are cleared up a bit?"

"No," wailed Winifred, her pent-up feelings breaking through all restraint. "I am quite alone in the world now."

"Come, come, cheer up!" said Steingall, rising and patting her on the shoulder. "This disagreeable business may only last a day or two. You will not want for anything. If you are in any trouble all you need do is to let me know. Moreover, to save you from being afraid of remaining alone in the house at night, I'll give special instructions to the police in your precinct to watch the place closely. Now, be a brave girl and make the best of it."

The house in One Hundred and Twelfth Street would, of course, be an object of special interest to the police for other reasons apart from those suggested by the chief. Nevertheless, his kindness had the desired effect, and Winifred strove to repress her tears.

"Here is your note," he said, "and I advise you to forget this temporary trouble in your work. Mr. Clancy will accompany you in the car if you wish."

"Please—I would rather be alone," she faltered. She was far from Mulberry Street before she remembered that she had said nothing about seeing the boat that morning!

CHAPTER V
PERSECUTORS

During the brief run up-town Winifred managed to dry her tears, yet the mystery and terror of the circumstances into which she was so suddenly plunged seemed to become more distressful the longer she puzzled over them. She could not find any outlet from a labyrinth of doubt and uncertainty. She strove again to read the printed accounts of the crime, in order to wrest from them some explanation of the extraordinary charge brought against her aunt, but the words danced before her eyes. At last, with an effort, she threw the paper away and bravely resolved to follow Steingall's parting advice.

When she reached the warehouse she was naturally the object of much covert observation. Neither Miss Sugg nor Mr. Fowle spoke to her, but Winifred thought she saw a malicious smile on the forewoman's face. The hours passed wearily until six o'clock. She was about to quit the building with her companions—many of whom meant bombarding her with questions at the first opportunity—when she was again requested to report at the office.

A clerk handed her one of the firm's pay envelopes.

"What's comin' to you up to date," he blurted out, "and a week's salary instead of notice."

She was dismissed!

Some girls might have collapsed under this final blow, but not so Winifred Bartlett. Knowing it was useless to say anything to the clerk, she spiritedly demanded an interview with the manager. This was refused. She insisted, and sent Steingall's letter to the inner sanctum, having concluded that the dismissal was in some way due to her visit to the detective bureau.

The clerk came back with the note and a message: "The firm desire me to tell you," he said, "that they quite accept your explanation, but they have no further need of your services."

Explanation! How could a humble employee explain away the unsavory fact that the smug respectability of Brown, Son & Brown had been outraged by the name of the firm appearing in the evening papers as connected, even in the remotest way, with the sensational crime now engaging the attention of all New York?

Winifred walked into the street. Something in her face warned even the most inquisitive of her fellow-workers to leave her alone. Besides, the poor always evince a lively sympathy with others in misfortune. These working-class girls were consumed with curiosity, yet they respected Winifred's feelings, and did not seek to intrude on her very apparent misery by inquiry or sympathetic condolence. A few among them watched, and even followed her a little way as she turned the corner into Fourteenth Street.

"She goes home by the Third Avenue L," said Carlotta. "Sometimes I've walked with her that far. H'lo! Why's Fowle goin' east in a taxi! He lives on West Seventeenth. Betcher a dime he's after Winnie."

"Whadda ya mean—after her?" cried another girl.

"Why, didn't you hear how he spoke up for her this mornin' when Ole Mother Sugg handed her the lemon about bein' late?"

"But he got her fired."

"G'wan!"

"He did, I tell you. I heard him phonin' a newspaper. He made 'em wise about Winnie's bein' pinched, and then took the paper to the boss. I was below with a packin' check when he went in, so I saw that with my own eyes, an' that's just as far as I'd trust Fowle."

The cynic's shrewd surmise was strictly accurate. Fowle had, indeed, secured Winifred's dismissal. Her beauty and disdain had stirred his lewd impulses to their depths. His plan now was to intercept her before she reached her home, and pose as the friend in need who is the most welcome of all friends. Knowing nothing whatsoever of her domestic surroundings he deemed it advisable to make inquiries on the spot. His crafty and vulpine nature warned him against running his head into a noose, since Winifred might own a strong-armed father or brother, but no one could possibly resent a well-meant effort at assistance.

The mere sight of her graceful figure as she hurried along with pale face and downcast eyes inflamed him anew when his taxi sped by. She could not avoid him now. He would go up-town by an earlier train, and await her at the corner of One Hundred and Twelfth Street.

But the wariest fox is apt to find his paw in a trap, and Fowle, though foxy, was by no means so astute as he imagined himself. Once again that day Fate was preparing a surprise for Winifred, and not the least dramatic feature thereof connoted the utter frustration and undoing of Fowle.

About the time that Winifred caught her train it befell that Rex Carshaw, gentleman of leisure, the most industrious idler who ever extracted dividends from a business he cared little about, drove a high-powered car across the Harlem River by the Willis Avenue Bridge, and entered that part of Manhattan which lies opposite Randall's Island.

This was a new world to the eyes of the young millionaire. Nor was it much to his liking. The mixed citizenry of New York must live somewhere, but Carshaw saw no reason why he and his dainty car should loiter in a district which seemed highly popular with all sorts of undesirable folks; so, after skirting Thomas Jefferson Park he turned west, meaning to reach the better roadway and more open stretches of Fifth Avenue.

A too hasty express wagon, however, heedless of the convenience of wealthy automobilists, bore down on Carshaw like a Juggernaut car, and straightway smashed the differential, besides inflicting other grievous injuries on a complex mechanism. A policeman, the proprietor of a neighboring garage, and a greatly interested crowd provided an impromptu jury for the dispute between Carshaw and the express man.

The latter put up a poor case. It consisted almost entirely of the bitter and oft-repeated plaint:

"What was a car like that doin' here, anyhow?"

The question sounded foolish. It was nothing of the kind. Only the Goddess of Wisdom could have answered it, and she, being invisible, was necessarily dumb.

At last, when the damaged car was housed for the night, Carshaw set out to walk a couple of blocks to the elevated railway, his main objective being dinner with his mother in their apartment on Madison Avenue. He found himself in a comparatively quiet street, wherein blocks of cheap modern flats alternated with the dingy middle-class houses of a by-gone generation. He halted to light a cigarette, and, at that moment, a girl of remarkable beauty passed, walking quickly, yet without apparent effort. She was pallid and agitated, and her eyes were swimming with ill-repressed tears.

As a matter of fact, Winifred nearly broke down at sight of her empty abode. It was a cheerless place at best, and now the thought of being left there alone had induced a sense of feminine helplessness which overcame her utterly.

Carshaw was distinctly impressed. In the first place, he was young and good-looking, and human enough to try and steal a second glance at such a lovely face, though the steadily decreasing light was not altogether favorable. Secondly, he thought he had never seen any girl who carried herself with such rhythmic grace. Thirdly, here was a woman in distress, and, to one of Carshaw's temperament and upbringing, that in itself formed a convincing reason why he should wish to help her.

He racked his brain for a fitting excuse to offer his services. He could find none. Above all else, Rex Carshaw was a gentleman.

Of course, he could not tell that the way was being made smooth for knight-errantry by a certain dragon named Fowle. He did not even quicken his pace, and was musing on the curious incongruity of the maid in distress with the rather squalid district in which she had her being when he saw a man bar her path.

This was Fowle, who, with lifted hat, was saying deferentially: "Miss Bartlett, may I have a word?"

Winifred stopped as though she had run into an unseen obstruction. She even recoiled a step or two.

"What do you want?" she said, and there was a quality of scorn, perhaps of fear, in her voice that sent Carshaw, now five yards away, into the open doorway of a block of flats. He was an impulsive young man. He liked the girl's face, and quite as fixedly disliked Fowle's. So he adopted the now world-famous policy of watchful waiting, being not devoid of a dim belief that the situation might evolve an overt act.

"I want to tell you how sorry I am for what happened to-day," said Fowle, trying to speak sympathetically, but not troubling to veil the bold admiration of his stare. "I tried hard to stop unpleasantness, and even risked a row with the boss. But it was no use. I couldn't do a thing."

"But why are you here?" demanded Winifred, and those sorrow-laden eyes of hers might have won pity from any but one of Fowle's order.

"To help, of course," came the ready assurance. "I can get you a far better job than stitchin' octavos at Brown's. You're not meanin' to stay home with your folks, I suppose?"

"That is kind of you," said Winifred. "I may have to depend altogether on my own efforts, so I shall need work. I'll write to you for a reference, and perhaps for advice."

She had unwittingly told Fowle just what he was eager to know—that she was friendless and alone. He prided himself on understanding the ways of women, and lost no more time in coming to the point.

"Listen, now, Winnie," he said, drawing nearer, "I'd like to see you through this worry. Forget it. You can draw down twice or three times the money as a model in Goldberg's Store. I know Goldberg, an' can fix things. An', say, why mope at home evenings? I often get orders for two for the theaters an' vaudeville shows. What about comin' along down-town to-night? A bit of dinner an' a cabaret'd cheer you up after to-day's unpleasantness."

Winifred grew scarlet with vexation. The man had always been a repulsive person in her eyes, and, unversed though she was in the world's wiles, she knew instinctively that his present pretensions were merely a cloak for rascality. One should be fair to Winifred, too. Like every other girl, she had pictured the Prince Charming who would come into her life some day. But—Fowle! Her gorge rose.

"How dare you follow me here and say such vile things?" she cried hysterically.

"What's up now?" said Fowle in mock surprise. "What have I said that you should fly off the trolley in that way?"

"I take it that this young lady is telling you to quit," broke in another voice. "Go, now! Go while the going is good."

Quietly but firmly elbowing Fowle aside, Rex Carshaw raised his hat and spoke to Winifred.

"If this fellow is annoying you he can soon be dealt with," he said. "Do you live near? If so, he can stop right here. I'll occupy his mind till you are out of sight."

The discomfited masher was snarling like a vicious cur. The first swift glance that measured the intruder's proportions did not warrant any display of active resentment on his part. Out of the tail of his eye, however, he noticed a policeman approaching on the opposite side of the street. The sight lent a confidence which might have been lacking otherwise.

"Why are you buttin' in?" he cried furiously. "This young lady is a friend of mine. I'm tryin' to pull her out of a difficulty, but she's got me all wrong. Anyhow, what business is it of yours?"

Fowle's anger was wasted, since Carshaw seemed not to hear. Indeed, why should a chivalrous young man pay heed to Fowle when he could gaze his fill into Winifred's limpid eyes and listen to her tuneful voice?

"I am very greatly obliged to you," she was saying, "but I hope Mr. Fowle understands now that I do not desire his company and will not seek to force it on me."

"Sure he understands. Don't you, Fowle?" and Carshaw gave the disappointed wooer a look of such manifest purpose that something had to happen quickly. Something did happen. Fowle knew the game was up, and behaved after the manner of his kind.

"You're a cute little thing, Winifred Bartlett," he sneered, with a malicious glance from the girl to Carshaw, while a coarse guffaw imparted venom to his utterance. "Think you're taking an easier road to the white lights, I guess?"

"Guess again, Fowle," said Carshaw.

He spoke so quietly that Fowle was misled, because the pavement rose and struck him violently on the back of his head. At least, that was his first impression. The second and more lasting one was even more disagreeable. When he sat up, and fumbled to recover his hat, he was compelled to apply a handkerchief to his nose, which seemed to have been reduced to a pulp.

"Too bad you should be mixed up in this disturbance," Carshaw was assuring Winifred, "but a pup of the Fowle species can be taught manners in only one way. Now, suppose you hurry home!"

The advice was well meant, and Winifred acted on it at once. Fowle had scrambled to his feet and the policeman was running up. From east and west a crowd came on the scene like a well-trained stage chorus rushing in from the wings.

"Now, then, what's the trouble?" demanded the law, with gruff insistency.

"Nothing. A friend of mine met with a slight accident—that's all," said Carshaw.

"It's—it's—all right," agreed Fowle thickly. Some glimmer of reason warned him that an exposé in the newspapers would cost him his job with Brown, Son & Brown. The policeman eyed the damaged nose. He grinned.

"If you care to take a wallop like that as a friendly tap it's your affair, not mine," he said. "Anyhow, beat it, both of you!"

Carshaw was not interested in Fowle or the policeman. He had been vouchsafed one expressive look by Winifred as she hurried away, and he watched the slim figure darting up half a dozen steps to a small brown-stone house, and opening the door with a latch-key. Oddly enough, the policeman's attention was drawn by the girl's movements. His air changed instantly.

"H'lo," he said, evidently picking on Fowle as the doubtful one of these two. "This must be inquired into. What's your name?"

"No matter. I make no charge."

Fowle was turning away, but the policeman grabbed him.

"You come with me to the station-house," he said determinedly. "An' you, too," he added jerking his head at Carshaw.

"Have you gone crazy with the heat?" inquired Carshaw.

"I hold you for fighting in the public street, an' that's all there is to it," was the firm reply. "You can come quietly or be 'cuffed, just as you like. Clear off, the rest of you."

An awe-stricken mob backed hastily. Fowle was too dazed even to protest, and Carshaw sensed some hidden but definite motive behind the policeman's strange alternation of moods. He looked again at the brown-stone house, but night was closing in so rapidly that he could not distinguish a face at any of the windows.

"Let us get there quickly—I'll be late for dinner," he said, and the three returned by the way Carshaw had come.

Thus it was that Rex Carshaw, eligible young society bachelor, was drawn into the ever-widening vortex of "The Yacht Mystery." He did not recognize it yet, but was destined soon to feel the force of its swirling currents.

Gazing from a window of the otherwise deserted house Winifred saw both her assailant and her protector marched off by the policeman. It was patent, even to her benumbed wits, that they had been arrested. The tailing-in of the mob behind the trio told her as much.

She was too stunned to do other than sink into a chair. For a while she feared she was going to faint. With lack-lustre eyes she peered into a gulf of loneliness and despair. Then outraged nature came to her aid, and she burst into a storm of tears.

CHAPTER VI
BROTHER RALPH.

Clancy forced Senator Meiklejohn's hand early in the fray. He was at the Senator's flat within an hour of the time Ronald Tower was dragged into the Hudson, but a smooth-spoken English man-servant assured the detective that his master was out, and not expected home until two or three in the morning.

This arrangement obviously referred to the Van Hofen festivity, so Clancy contented himself with asking the valet to give the Senator a card on which he scribbled a telephone number and the words, "Please ring up when you get this."

Now, he knew, and Senator Meiklejohn knew, the theater at which Mrs. Tower was enjoying herself. He did not imagine for an instant that the Senator was discharging the mournful duty of announcing to his friend's wife the lamentable fate which had overtaken her husband. Merely as a perfunctory duty he went to the theater and sought the manager.

"You know Mrs. Ronald Tower?" he said.

"Sure I do," said the official. "She's inside now. Came here with Bobby Forrest."

"Anybody called for her recently?"

"I think not, but I'll soon find out."

No. Mrs. Tower's appreciation of Belasco's genius had not been disturbed that evening.

"Anything wrong?" inquired the manager.

Clancy's answer was ready.

"If Senator Meiklejohn comes here within half an hour, see that the lady is told at once," he said. "If he doesn't show up in that time, send for Mr. Forrest, tell him that Mr. Tower has met with an accident, and leave him to look after the lady."

"Wow! Is it serious? Why wait?"

"The slight delay won't matter, and the Senator can handle the situation better than Forrest."

Clancy gave some telephonic instruction to the man on night duty at headquarters. He even dictated a paragraph for the press. Then he went straight to bed, for the hardiest detectives must sleep, and he had a full day's work before him when next the sun rose over New York.

He summed up Meiklejohn's action correctly. The Senator did not communicate with Mulberry Street during the night, so Clancy was an early visitor at his apartment.

"The Senator is ill and can see no one," said the valet.

"No matter how ill he may be, he must see me," retorted Clancy.

"But he musn't be disturbed. I have my orders."

"Take a fresh set. He's going to be disturbed right now, by you or me. Choose quick!"

The law prevailed. A few minutes later Senator Meiklejohn entered the library sitting-room, where the little detective awaited him. He looked wretchedly ill, but his sufferings were mental, not physical. Examined critically now, in the cold light of day, he was a very different man from the spruce, dandified politician and financier who figured so prominently among Van Hofen's guests the previous evening. Yet Clancy saw at a glance that the Senator was armed at all points. Diplomacy would be useless. The situation demanded a bludgeon. He began the attack at once.

"Why didn't you ring up Mulberry Street last night, Senator?" he said.

"I was too upset. My nerves were all in."

"You told the patrolman at Eighty-sixth Street that you were hurrying away to break the news to Mrs. Tower, yet you did not go near her?"

Meiklejohn affected to consult Clancy's card to ascertain the detective's name.

"Perhaps I had better get in touch with the Bureau now," he said, and a flush of anger darkened his haggard face.

"No need. The Bureau is right here. Let us get down to brass tacks, Senator. A woman named Rachel met you outside the Four Hundred Club at eight o'clock as you were coming out. You had just spoken to Mrs. Tower, when this woman told you that you must meet two men who would await you at the Eighty-sixth landing-stage at nine. You were to bring five hundred dollars. At nine o'clock these same men killed Mr. Tower, and you yourself admitted to me that they mistook him for you. Now, will you be good enough to fill in the blanks? Who is Rachel? Where does she live? Who were the two men? Why should you give them five hundred dollars, apparently as blackmail?"

Clancy was exceedingly disappointed by the result of this thunderbolt. Any ordinary man would have shrivelled under its crushing impact. If the police knew so much that might reasonably be regarded as secret, of what avail was further concealment? Yet Senator Meiklejohn bore up wonderfully. He showed surprise, as well he might, but was by no means pulverized.

"All this is rather marvelous," he said slowly, after a long pause. He had avoided Clancy's gaze after the first few words, and sank into an armchair with an air of weariness that was not assumed.

"Simple enough," commented the detective readily. Above all else he wanted Meiklejohn to talk. "I was on duty outside the club, and heard almost every word that passed between you and Rachel."

"Well, well."

The Senator arose and pressed an electric bell.

"If you don't mind," he explained suavely, "I'll order some coffee and rolls. Will you join me?"

This was the parry of a skilled duelist to divert an attack and gain breathing-time. Clancy rather admired such adroitness.

"Sorry, I can't on principle," he countered.

"How — on principle?"

"You see, Senator, I may have to arrest you, and I never eat with any man with whom I may clash professionally."

"You take risks, Mr. Clancy."

"I love 'em. I'd cut my job to-day if it wasn't for the occasional excitement."

The valet appeared.

"Coffee and rolls for two, Phillips," said Meiklejohn. He turned to Clancy. "Perhaps you would prefer toast and an egg?"

"I have breakfasted already, Senator," smiled the detective, "but I may dally with the coffee."

When the door was closed on Phillips, his master glanced at a clock on the mantelpiece. The hour was eight-fifteen. Some days elapsed before Clancy interpreted that incident correctly.

"You rose early," said the Senator.

"Yes, but worms are coy this morning."

"Meaning that you still await answers to your questions. I'll deal with you fully and frankly, but I'm curious to know on what conceivable ground you could arrest me for the murder of my friend Ronald Tower."

"As an accessory before the act."

"But, consider. You have brains, Mr. Clancy. I am glad the Bureau sent such a man. How can a bit of unthinking generosity on my part be construed as participation in a crime?"

"If you explain matters, Senator, the absurdity of the notion may become clear."

"Ah, that's better. Let me assure you that my coffee will not affect your fine sensibilities. Miss Rachel Craik is a lady I have known nearly all my life. I have assisted her, within my means. She resides in East One Hundred and Twelfth Street, and the man about whom she was so concerned last night is her brother. He committed some technical offense years ago, and has always been a ne'er-do-well. To please his sister, and for no other reason, I undertook to provide him with five hundred dollars, and thus enable him to start life anew. I have never met the man. I would not recognize him if I saw him. I believe he is a desperate character; his maniacal behavior last night seems to leave no room for doubt in that respect. Don't you see, Mr. Clancy, that it was I, and not poor Tower, whom he meant attacking? But for idle chance, it is my corpse, not Tower's, that would now be floating in the Hudson. You heard what Tower said. I did not. I assume, however, that some allusion was made to the money—which, by the way, is still in my pocketbook—and Tower scoffed at the notion that he had come there to hand over five hundred dollars. There you have the whole story, in so far as I can tell it."

"For the present, Senator."

"How?"

"It should yield many more chapters. Is that all you're going to say? For instance, did you call on Rachel Craik after leaving Eighty-sixth Street?"

Meiklejohn's jaws closed like a steel trap. He almost lost his temper.

"No," he said, seemingly conquering the desire to blaze into anger at this gadfly of a detective.

"Sure?"

"I said 'no.' That is not 'yes.' I was so overcome by Tower's miserable fate that I dismissed my car and walked home. I could not face any one, least of all Helen—Mrs. Tower."

"Or the Bureau?"

"Mr. Clancy, you annoy me."

Clancy stood up.

"I must duck your coffee, Senator," he said cheerfully. "Is Miss Craik on the phone?"

"No. She is poor, and lives alone—or, to be correct, with a niece, I believe."

"Well, think matters over. I'll see you again soon. Then you may be able to tell me some more."

"I have told you everything."

"Perhaps *I* may do the telling."

"Now, as to this poor woman, Miss Craik. You will not adopt harsh measures, I trust?"

"We are never harsh, Senator. If she speaks the truth, and all the truth, she need not fear."

In the hall Clancy met the valet, carrying a laden tray.

"Do you make good coffee, Phillips?" he inquired.

"I try to," smiled the other.

"Ah, that's modest—that's the way real genius speaks. Sorry I can't sample your brew to-day. So few Englishmen know the first thing about coffee."

"Nice, friendly little chap," was Phillips's opinion of the detective. Senator Meiklejohn's description of the same person was widely different. When Clancy went out, he, too, rose and stretched his stiff limbs.

"I got rid of that little rat more easily than I expected," he mused—that is to say, the Senator's thoughts may be estimated in some such phrase. But he was grievously mistaken in his belief. Clancy was no rat, but a most stubborn terrier when there were rats around.

While Meiklejohn was drinking his coffee the telephone rang. It was Mrs. Tower. She was heartbroken, or professed to be, since no more selfish woman existed in New York.

"Are you coming to see me?" she wailed.

"Yes, yes, later in the day. At present I dare not. I am too unhinged. Oh, Helen, what a tragedy! Have you any news?"

"News! My God! What news can I hope for except that Ronald's poor, maimed body has been found?"

"Helen, this is terrible. Bear up!"

"I'm doing my best. I can hardly believe that this thing has really happened. Help me in one small way, Senator. Telephone Mr. Jacob and explain why our luncheon is postponed."

"Yes, I'll do that."

Meiklejohn smiled grimly as he hung up the receiver. In the midst of her tribulations Helen Tower had not forgotten Jacob and the little business of the Costa Rica Cotton Concession! The luncheon was only "postponed."

An inquiry came from a newspaper, whereupon he gave a curt order that no more calls were to be made that day, as the apartment would be empty. He dressed, and devoted himself forthwith to the task of overhauling papers. He had a fire kindled in the library.

Hour after hour he worked, until the grate was littered with the ashes of destroyed documents. Sending for newspapers, he read of Rachel Craik's arrest. At last, when the light waned, he looked at his watch. Should he not face his fellow-members at the Four Hundred Club? Would it not betray weakness to shirk the ordeal of inquiry, of friendly scrutiny and half-spoken wonder that he, the irreproachable, should be mixed up in such a weird tragedy. Once he sought support from a decanter of brandy.

"Confound it!" he muttered, "why am I so shaky. *I* didn't murder Tower. My whole life may be ruined by one false step!"

He was still pondering irresolutely a visit to the club when Phillips came. The valet seemed flurried.

"There's a gentleman outside, sir, who insists on seeing you," he said nervous-

BROTHER RALPH.

ly. "He's a very violent gentleman, sir. He said if I didn't announce him he— —"

"What name?" interrupted Meiklejohn.

"Name of Voles, sir."

"Voles?"

"Yes, sir, but he says you'll recognize him better by the initials R. V. V."

Men of Meiklejohn's physique—big, fleshy, with the stamp of success on them—are rare subjects for nervous attacks. They seem to defy events which will shock the color out of ordinary men's cheeks, yet Meiklejohn felt that if he dared encounter the eyes of his discreet servant he would do something outrageous—shriek, or jump, or tear his hair. He bent over some papers on the table.

"Send Mr. Voles in," he murmured. "If any other person calls, say I'm engaged."

The man who was ushered into the room was of a stature and demeanor which might well have cowed the valet. Tall, strongly built, altogether fitter and more muscular than the stalwart Senator, he carried with him an impression of truculence, of a savage forcefulness, not often clothed in the staid garments of city life. Were his skin bronze, were he decked in the barbaric trappings of a Pawnee chief, his appearance would be more in accord with the chill and repellant significance of his personality. His square, hard features might have been chiseled out of granite. A pair of singularly dark eyes blazed beneath heavy and prominent eyebrows. A high forehead, a massive chin, and a well-shaped nose lent a certain intellectuality to the face, but this attribute was negatived by the coarse lines of a brutal mouth.

From any point of view the visitor must invite attention, while compelling dislike—even fear. In a smaller frame, such qualities might escape recognition, but this man's giant physique accentuated the evil aspect of eyes and mouth. Hardly waiting till the door was closed, he laughed sarcastically.

"You are well fixed here, brother o' mine," he said.

The man whom he addressed as "brother" leaned with his hands on the table that separated them. His face was quite ghastly. All his self-control seemed to have deserted him.

"You?" he gasped. "To come here! Are you mad?"

"Need you ask? It will not be the first time you have called me a lunatic, nor will it be the last, I reckon."

"But the risk, the infernal risk! The police know of you. Rachel is arrested. A detective was here a few hours ago. They are probably watching outside."

"Bosh!" was the uncompromising answer. "I'm sick of being hunted. Just for a change I turn hunter. Where's the mazuma you promised Rachel?"

Meiklejohn, using a hand like one in a palsy, produced a pocketbook and took from it a bundle of notes.

"Here!" he quavered. "Now, for Heaven's sake——"

"Just the same old William," cried the stranger, seating himself unceremoniously. "Always ready to do a steal, but terrified lest the law should grab him. No, I'm not going. It will be good nerve tonic for you to sit down and talk while you strain your ears to hear the tramp of half a dozen cops in the hall. What a poor fish you are!" he continued, voice and manner revealing a candid contempt, as Meiklejohn did indeed start at the slamming of a door somewhere in the building. "Do you think I'd risk my neck if I were likely to be pinched? Gad! I know my way around too well for that."

"But you don't understand," whispered the other in mortal terror. "By some means the detective bureau may know of your existence. Rachel promised to be close-lipped, but—"

"Oh, take a bracer out of that decanter. At the present moment I am registered in a big Fifth Avenue hotel, a swell joint which they wouldn't suspect in twenty years."

"How can that be? Rachel said you were in desperate need."

"So I was until I went through that idiot's pockets. He had two hundred dollars in bills and chicken-feed. I knew I'd get another wad from you to-night."

"Why did you want to murder me, Ralph?"

"Murder! Oh, shucks! I didn't want to kill anybody. But I don't trust you, William. I'm always expecting you to double-cross me. Last night it was a lasso. To-night it is this." And he suddenly whipped out a revolver.

CHAPTER VII
STILL MERE MYSTERY

Meiklejohn pushed his chair back so quickly that it caught the fender and brought down some fire-irons with a crash.

"More nerves!" croaked his grim-visaged relative, but the revolver disappeared.

"Tell me," said the tortured Meiklejohn; "why have you returned to New York? Above all, why did you straightway commit a crime that cannot fail to stir the whole country?"

"That's better. You are showing some sort of brotherly interest. I came back because I was sick of mining camps and boundless sierras. I had a hankering after the old life—the theaters, dinners, race-meetings, wine and women. As to 'the crime,' I thought that fool was you. He called for the cops."

"For the police! Why?"

"Because my line of talk was a trifle too rough, I suppose."

"Did he know you were there to meet me?"

"Can't say. The whole thing was over like a flash. I am quick on the trigger."

"But if you had killed me what other goose would lay golden eggs?"

"You forget that the goose was unwilling to lay any more eggs. I only meant scaring you. To haul you neck and crop into the river was a good scheme. You see, we haven't met for some years."

"Then why—why murder Ronald Tower?"

"There you go again. Murder! How you chew on the word. I never touched the man, only to haul him into the boat and go through his pockets. I guess he had a weak heart, due to over-eating, and the cold water upset him."

"But you left him in the river?"

"Wrong every time. I chucked him into a barge and covered him tenderly with a tarpaulin."

Meiklejohn sprang upright. "Good God," he cried, "he may be alive!"

"Sit down, William, sit down," was the cool response. "If he's alive, he'll turn up. In any case, he'll be found sooner or later. Shout the glad news now and you go straight to the Tombs."

This was obviously so true that the Senator collapsed into his chair again, and in so doing disturbed the fire-irons a second time.

The incident amused the unbidden guest. "I see you won't be happy till I leave you," he laughed, "so let's go on with the knitting. That girl—she is becoming a woman—what is to be done with her?"

"Rachel takes every care—"

"Rachel is excellent in her way. But she is growing old. She may die. The girl is the living image of her mother. It's a queer world, and a small one at times. For instance, who would have expected your double to walk onto the terrace at the landing-stage at nine o'clock precisely last night? Well, some one may recognize the likeness. Inquiries might be instituted. That would be very awkward for you."

"Far more awkward for you."

"Not a bit of it. I've lived with my neck in the loop for eighteen years. I'm getting used to it. But you, William, with your Senatorship and high record in Wall Street—really the downfall would be terrible!"

"What can we do with her? Murder her, as you—"

"The devil take you and your parrotlike repetition of one word!" roared brother Ralph, bringing his clenched fist down on the table with a bang. "I never laid violent hands on a woman yet, whatever I may have done to men. Who has reaped the reward of my misdeeds, I'd like to know—I, an outcast and a wanderer, or you, living here like Lord Tomnoddy? None of your preaching to me, you smug Pharisee! We're six of one and half a dozen of the other."

When this self-proclaimed adventurer was really aroused he dropped the rough argot of the plains. His diction showed even some measure of culture.

Meiklejohn walked unsteadily to the door. He opened it. There was no one in the passage without.

"I'm sorry," he said in a strangely subdued voice. "What do you want? What do you suggest?"

"This," came the instant reply. "It was a piece of folly on Rachel's part to educate the girl the way she did. You stopped the process too late. In a year or two Miss Winifred will begin to think and ask questions, if she hasn't done so already. She must leave the East—better quit America altogether."

"Very well. When this affair of Tower's blows over I'll arrange it."

The other man seemed to be somewhat mollified. He lighted a cigarette. "That rope play was sure a mad trick," he conceded sullenly, "but I thought you were putting the cops on my trail."

A bell rang and the Senator started. Many callers, mostly reporters, had been turned away by Phillips already that day, but brother Ralph's untimely visit had made the position peculiarly dangerous. Moreover, the valet's protests had proved unavailing this time. The two heard his approaching footsteps.

Meiklejohn's care-worn face turned almost green with fright, and even his hardier companion yielded to a sense of peril. He leaped up, moving catlike on his toes.

"Where does that door lead to?" he hissed, pointing.

"A bedroom. But I've given orders—"

"You dough-faced dub, don't you see you create suspicion by refusing to meet people? And, listen! If this is a cop, bluff hard! I'll shoot up the whole Bureau before they get me!"

He vanished, moving with a silence and celerity that were almost uncanny in so huge a man. Phillips knocked and thrust his head in. He looked scared yet profoundly relieved.

"Mr. Tower to see you, sir," he said breathlessly.

"What?" shrieked the Senator in a shrill falsetto.

"Yes, sir. It's Mr. Tower himself, sir."

"H'lo, Bill!" came a familiar voice. "Here I am! No spook yet, thank goodness!"

Meiklejohn literally staggered to the door and nearly fell into Ronald Tower's arms. Of the two men, the Senator seemed nearer death at that moment. He blubbered something incoherent, and had to be assisted to a chair. Even Tower was astonished at the evident depth of his friend's emotion.

"Cheer up, old sport!" he cried affectionately. "I had no notion you felt so badly about my untimely end, as the newspapers call it. I tried to get you on the phone, but you were closed down, the exchange said, so Helen packed me off here when she was able to sit up and take nourishment. Gad! Even my wife seems to have missed me!"

Many minutes elapsed before Senator Meiklejohn's benumbed brain could assimilate the facts of a truly extraordinary story. Tower, after being whisked so unceremoniously into the Hudson, remembered nothing further until he opened his eyes in numb semi-consciousness in the cubbyhole of a tug plodding through the long Atlantic rollers off the New Jersey coast.

When able to talk he learned that the captain of the tug *Cygnet*, having received orders to tow three loaded barges from a Weehawken pier to Barnegat City, picked up his "job" at nine-thirty the previous night, and dropped down the river with the tide. In the early morning he was amazed by the sight of a man crawling from under the heavy tarpaulin that sheeted one of the barges—a man so dazed and weak that he nearly fell into the sea.

"Cap' Rickards slowed up and took me aboard," explained Tower volubly. "Then he filled me with rock and rye and packed me in blankets. Gee, how they smelt, but how grateful they were! What between prime old whiskey inside and greasy wool outside I dodged a probable attack of pneumonia. When the *Cygnet* tied up at Barnegat at noon to-day I was fit as a fiddle. Cap' Rickards rigged me out in his shore-going suit and lent me twenty dollars, as that pair of blackguards in the launch had robbed me of every cent. They even took a crooked sixpence I found in London twenty years ago, darn 'em! I phoned Helen, of course, but didn't realize what a hubbub my sad fate had created until I read a newspaper in the train. When I reached home poor Helen was so out of gear that she hadn't told a soul of my escape. I do believe she hardly accepted my own assurance that I was still on the map. However, when I got her calmed down a bit, she remembered you and the rest of the excitement, so I phoned the detective bureau and the club, and came straight here."

"That is very good of you, Tower," murmured Meiklejohn brokenly. He looked in far worse plight than the man who had survived such a desperate adventure.

"Well, my dear chap, I was naturally anxious to see you, because—but perhaps you don't know that those scoundrels meant to attack you, not me?"

Meiklejohn smiled wanly. "Oh, yes," he said. "The police found that out by some means. I believe the authorities actually suspected me of being concerned in the affair."

Tower laughed boisterously. "That's the limit!" he roared. "Come with me to the club. We'll soon spoil that yarn. What a fuss the papers made! I'm quite a celebrity."

"I'll follow you in half an hour. And, look here, Tower, this matter did really affect me. There was a woman in the case. I butted into an old feud merely as a friend. I think matters will now be settled amicably. Allow me to make good your loss in every way. If you can persuade the police that the whole thing was a hoax—"

For the first time Tower looked non-plussed. He was enjoying the notoriety thrust on him so unexpectedly.

"Well, I can hardly do that," he said. "But if I can get them to drop further inquiries I'll do it, Meiklejohn, for your sake. Gee! Come to look at you, you must have had a bad time.... Well, good-by, old top! See you later. Suppose we dine together? That will help dissipate this queer story as to you being mixed up in an attack on me. Now, I must be off and play ghost in the club smoking-room."

Meiklejohn heard his fluttering man-servant let Tower out. He tottered to a chair, and Ralph Voles came in noiselessly.

"Well, what about it?" chuckled the reprobate. "We seem to have struck it lucky."

"Go away!" snarled the Senator, goaded to a sudden rage by the other man's cynical humor. "I can stand no more to-day."

"Oh, take a pull at this!" And the decanter was pushed across the table. "Didn't Dr. Johnson once say that claret is the liquor for boys, port for men, but he who aspires to be a hero should drink brandy? And you must be a hero to-night. Get onto the Bureau and use the soft pedal. Then beat it to the club. You and Tower ought to be well soused in an hour. He's a good sport, all right. I'll mail him that sixpence if it's still in my pants."

"Do nothing of the sort!" snapped Meiklejohn. "You're—"

"Ah, cut it out! Tower wants plenty to talk about. His crooked sixpence will fill many an eye, and the more he spiels the better it is for you. Gee, but you're yellow for a two-hundred pounder! Now, listen! Make those cops drop all charges against Rachel. Then, in a week or less, I'll come along and fix things about the girl. She's the fly in the amber now. Mind she doesn't get out, or the howl about Mr. Ronald Tower's trip to Barnegat won't amount to a row of beans against the trouble pretty Winifred can give you. *Dios!* It's a pity. She's a real beauty, and that's more than any one can say for you, Brother William."

"You go to—"

"That's better! You're reviving. Well, good-by, Senator! *Au revoir sans adieux!*"

The big man swaggered out. Meiklejohn drank no spirits. He needed a clear brain that evening. After deep self-communing he rang up police headquarters and inquired for Mr. Clancy.

"Mr. Clancy is out," he was told by some one with a strong, resonant voice. "Anything we can do, Senator?"

"About that poor woman, Rachel Craik—"

"Oh, she's all right! She gave us a farewell smile two hours ago."

"You mean she is at liberty?"

"Certainly, Senator."

"May I ask to whom I am speaking?"

"Steingall, Chief of the Bureau."

"This wretched affair—it's merely a family squabble between Miss Craik and a relative—might well end now, Mr. Steingall."

"That is for Mr. Tower and Mr. Van Hofen to decide."

"Yes, I quite understand. I have seen Mr. Tower, and he shares my opinion."

"Just so, Senator. At any rate, the yacht mystery is almost cleared up."

"I agree with you most heartily."

For the first time in nearly twenty-four hours Senator Meiklejohn looked contented with life when he hung up the receiver. Therefore, it was well for his peace of mind that he could not hear Steingall's silent comment as he, in turn, disconnected the phone.

"That old fox agreed with me too heartily," he thought. "The yacht mystery is only just beginning—or I'm a Dutchman!"

CHAPTER VIII
THE DREAM FACE

That evening of her dismissal from Brown's, and her meeting with Rex Carshaw, Winifred opened the door of the dun house in One Hundred and Twelfth Street the most downhearted girl in New York. Suddenly, mystery had gathered round her. Something threatened, she knew not what. When the door slammed behind her her heart sank—she was alone not only in the house, but in the world. This thought possessed her utterly when the excitement caused by Carshaw and Fowle, and their speedy arrest, had passed.

That her aunt, the humdrum Rachel Craik, should have any sort of connection with the murder of Ronald Tower, of which Winifred had chanced first to hear on Riverside Drive that morning, seemed the wildest nonsense. Then Winifred was overwhelmed afresh, and breathed to herself, "I must be dreaming!"

And yet—the house was empty! Her aunt was not there—her aunt was held as a criminal! It was not a dream, but only like one, a waking nightmare far more terrifying. Most of the rooms in the house had nothing but dust in them. Rachel Craik had preferred to live as solitary in teeming Manhattan as a castaway on a rock in the midst of the sea.

Winifred's mind was accustomed now to the thought of that solitude shared by two. This night, when there were no longer two, but only one, the question arose strongly in her mind—why had there never been more than two? Certainly her aunt was not rich, and might well have let some of the rooms. Yet, even the suggestion of such a thing had made Rachel Craik angry. This, for the first time, struck Winifred as odd. Everything was puzzling, and all sorts of doubts peeped up in her, like ghosts questioning her with their eyes in the dark.

When the storm of tears had spent its force she had just enough interest in her usual self to lay the table and make ready a meal, but not enough interest to eat it. She sat by a window of her bedroom, her hat still on her head, looking down. The street lamps were lit. It grew darker and darker. Down there below feet passed and repassed in multitudes, like drops of the eternal cataract of life.

Winifred's eyes rested often on the spot where Rex Carshaw had spoken to her and had knocked down Fowle, her tormentor. In hours of trouble, when the mind is stunned, it will often go off into musings on trivial things. So this young girl, sitting at the window of the dark and empty house, let her thoughts wander to her rescuer. He was well built, and poised like an athlete. He had a quick step, a quick way of talking, was used to command; his brow was square, and could threaten; he had the deepest blue eyes, and glossy brown hair; he was a tower of strength to protect a girl; and his wife, if he had one, must have a feeling of safety. Thoughts, or half-thoughts, like these passed through her mind. She had never before met any young man of Carshaw's type.

It became ten o'clock. She was tired after the day's work and trouble of mind. The blow of her dismissal, the fright of her interview with the police, the arrest of her aunt—all this sudden influx of mystery and care formed a burden from which there was no escape for exhausted nature but in sleep. Her eyes grew weary at last, and, getting up, she discarded her hat and some of her clothes; then threw herself on the bed, still half-dressed, and was soon asleep.

The hours of darkness rolled on. That tramp of feet in the street grew thin and scattered, as if the army of life had undergone a repulse. Then there was a rally, when the theaters and picture-houses poured out their crowds; but it was short, the powers of night were in the ascendant, and soon the last stragglers retreated under cover. Of all this Winifred heard nothing—she slept soundly.

But was it in a dream, that voice which she heard? Something somewhere seemed to whisper, "She must be taken out of New York—she is the image of her mother."

It was a hushed, grim voice.

The room, the whole house, had been in darkness when she had thrown herself on the bed. But, somewhere, had she not been conscious of a light at some moment? Had she dreamed this, or had she seen it? She sat up in bed, staring and startled. The room was in darkness. In her ears were the words: "She is the image of her mother."

She had heard them in some world, she did not know in which. She listened with the keen ears of fear. Not a wagon nor a taxi any longer moved in the street; no step passed; the house was silent.

But after a long ten minutes the darkness seemed to become pregnant with a sound, a steady murmur. It was as if it came from far away, as if a brook had spurted out of the granite of Manhattan, and was even more like a dream-sound than those words which still buzzed in Winifred's ear. Somehow that murmur as of water in the night made Winifred think of a face, one which, as far as she could remember, she had never consciously seen—a man's face, brown, hard, and menacing, which had looked once into her eyes in some state of semi-conscious being, and then had vanished. And now this question arose in her mind: was it not that face, hard and brown, which she had never seen, and yet once had seen—were not those the cruel lips which somewhere had whispered: "She is the image of her mother?"

Winifred, sitting up in bed, listened to the steady, dull murmuring a long time, till there came a moment when she said definitely: "It is in the house."

For, as her ears grew accustomed to its tone, it seemed to lose some of its remoteness, to become more local and earthly. Presently this sound which the darkness was giving out became the voices of people talking in subdued undertones not far off. Nor was it long before the murmur was broken by a word sharply uttered and clearly heard by her—a gruff and unmistakable oath. She started with fright at this, it sounded so near. She was certain now that there were others in the house with her. She had gone to bed alone. Waking up in the dead of the small hours to find men or ghosts with her, her heart beat horribly.

But ghosts do not swear—at least such was Winifred's ideal of the spirit world. And she was brave. Nerving herself for the ordeal, she found the courage to steal out of bed and make her way out of the room into a passage, and she had not stood there listening two minutes when she was able to be certain that the murmur was going on in a back room.

How earnest that talk was—how low in pitch! It could hardly be burglars there, for burglars do not enter a house in order to lay their heads together in long conferences. It could not be ghosts, for a light came out under the rim of the door.

After a time Winifred stole forward, tapped on a panel, and her heart jumped into her mouth as she lifted her voice, saying:

"Aunty, is it you?"

There was silence at this, as though they had been ghosts, indeed, and had taken to flight at the breath of the living.

"Speak! Who is it?" cried Winifred with a fearful shrillness now. A chair grated on the floor inside, hurried steps were heard, a key turned, the door opened a very little, and Winifred saw the gaunt face of Rachel Craik looking dourly at her, for she had frightened this masterful woman very thoroughly.

"Oh, aunt, it *is* you!" gasped Winifred with a flutter of relief.

"You are to go to bed, Winnie," said Rachel.

"It is you! They have let you out, then?"

"Yes."

"Tell me what happened; let me come in—"

"Go back to bed; there's a good girl. I'll tell you everything in the morning."

"Oh, but I am glad! I was so lonely and frightened! Aunt, what was it all about?"

"About nothing; as far as I can discover," said Rachel Craik—"a mere mare's-nest found by a set of stupid police. Some man—a Mr. Ronald Tower—was supposed to have been murdered, and I was supposed to have some connection with it, though I had never seen the creature in my life. Now the man has turned up safe and sound, and the pack of noodles have at last thought fit to allow a respectable woman to come home to her bed."

"Oh, how good! Thank heaven! But, you have some one in there with you?"

"In here—where?"

"Why, in the room, aunt."

"I? No, no one."

"I am sure I heard—"

"Now, really, you must go to bed, Winifred! What are you doing awake at this hour of the morning, roaming about the house? You were asleep half an hour ago—"

"Oh, then, it was your light I saw in my sleep! I thought I heard a man say: 'She is the image—'"

"Just think of troubling me with your dreams at this unearthly hour! I'm tired, child; go to bed."

"Yes—but, aunt, this day's work has cost me my situation. I am dismissed!"

"Well, a holiday will do you good."

"Good gracious—you take it coolly!"

"Go to bed."

A sudden din of tumbling weights and splintering wood broke out behind the half-open door. For, within the room a man had been sitting on a chair tilted back on its two hind legs. The chair was old and slender, the man huge; and one of the chair-legs had collapsed under the weight and landed the man on the floor.

"Oh, aunt! didn't you say that no one—" began Winifred.

The sentence was never finished. Rachel Craik, her features twisted in anger, pushed the young girl with a force which sent her staggering, and then immediately shut the door. Winifred was left outside in the darkness.

She returned to her bed, but not to sleep. It was certain that her aunt had lied to her—there was more in the air than Winifred's quick wits could fathom. The fact of Rachel Craik's release did not clear up the mystery of the fact that she had been arrested. Winifred lay, spurring her fancy to account for all that puzzled her; and underlying her thoughts was the man's face and those strange words which she had heard somewhere on the borders of sleep.

She fancied she had seen the man somewhere before. At last she recalled the occasion, and almost laughed at the conceit. It was a picture of Sitting Bull, and that eminent warrior had long since gone to the happy hunting-grounds.

Meantime, the murmur of voices in the back room had recommenced and was going on. Then, towards morning, Winifred became aware that the murmur had stopped, and soon afterward she heard the click of the lock of the front door and a foot going down the front steps.

Rising quickly, she crept to the window and looked out. Going from the door down the utterly empty street she saw a man, a big swaggerer, with something of the over-seas and the adventurer in his air. It was Ralph "Voles," the "brother" of Senator William Meiklejohn. But Winifred could not distinguish his features, or she might have recognized the man she had seen in her half-dreams, and who had said: "She must be taken out of New York—she is the image of her mother."

Voles had hardly quitted the place before a street-car conductor, who had taken temporary lodgings the previous evening in a house opposite, hurried out into the coldness of the hour before dawn. He seemed pleased at the necessity of going to work thus early.

"Oh, boy!" he said softly. "I'm glad there's somethin' doin' at last. I was getting that sleepy. I could hardly keep me eyes open!"

When Detective Clancy came to the Bureau a few hours later he found a memorandum to the effect that a Mr. Ralph V. Voles, of Chicago, stopping at a high-grade hotel in Fifth Avenue, had dined with Rachel Craik in a quiet restaurant, had parted from her, and met her again, evidently by appointment. The two had entered the house in One Hundred and Twelfth Street separately shortly before midnight, and Voles returned to his hotel at four o'clock in the morning.

Clancy shook his head waggishly.

"Who'd have thought it of you, Rachel?" he cackled. "And, now that I've seen *you*, what sort of weird specimen can Mr. Ralph V. Voles, of Chicago, be? I'll look him up!"

CHAPTER IX
THE FLIGHT

Carshaw and Fowle enjoyed, let us say, a short but almost triumphal march to the nearest police-station. Their escort of loafers and small boys grew quickly in numbers and enthusiasm. It became known that the arrest was made in East One Hundred and Twelfth Street, and that street had suddenly become famous. The lively inhabitants of the East Side do not bother their heads about grammatical niceties, so the gulf between "the yacht murder" and "the yacht murderers" was easily bridged. The connection was clear. Two men in a boat, and two men in the grip of the law! It needed only Fowle's ensanguined visage to complete the circle of reasoning. Consciousness of this ill-omened popularity infuriated Carshaw and alarmed Fowle. When they arrived at the precinct station-house each was inclined to wish he had never seen or heard of Winifred Bartlett!

Their treatment by the official in charge only added fuel to the flame. The patrolman explained that "these two were fighting about the girl who lives in that house in East One Hundred and Twelfth," and this vague statement seemed all-sufficient. The sergeant entered their names and addresses. He went to the telephone and came back.

"Sit there!" he said authoritatively, and they sat there, Carshaw trying to take an interest in a "drunk" who was brought in, and Fowle alternately feeling the sore lump at the back of his head and the sorer cartilage of his nose. After waiting half an hour Carshaw protested, but the sergeant assured him that "a man from the Bureau" was *en route* and would appear presently. At last Clancy came in. That is why he was "out" when Senator Meiklejohn inquired for him.

"H'lo!" he cried when he set eyes on Fowle. "My foreman bookbinder! Your folio looks somewhat battered!"

"Glad it's you, Mr. Clancy," snuffled Fowle. "You can tell these cops—"

"Suppose *you* tell me," broke in the detective, with a glance at Carshaw.

"Yes, Fowle, speak up," said Carshaw. "You've a ready tongue. Explain your fall from grace."

"There's nothing to it," growled Fowle. "I know the girl, an' asked her to come with me this evening. She'd been fired by the firm, an'—"

"Ah! Who fired her?" Clancy's inquiry sounded most matter-of-fact.

"The boss, of course."

"Why?"

"Well—this newspaper stuff. He didn't like it."

"He told you so?"

"Yes. That is—the department is a bit crowded. He—er—asked me—Well, we reckoned we could do without her."

"I see. Go on."

"So I just came up-town, meanin' to talk things over, an' find her a new job, but she took it all wrong."

Clancy whirled around on Carshaw. Evidently he had heard enough from Fowle.

"And you?" he snapped.

"I know nothing of either party," was the calm answer. "I couldn't help overhearing this fellow insulting a lady, so put him where he belongs—in the gutter."

"Mr. Clancy," interrupted the sergeant, "you're wanted on the phone."

The detective was detained a good five minutes. When he returned he walked straight up to Fowle.

"Quit!" he said, with a scornful and sidelong jerk of the head. "You got what you wanted. Get out, and leave Miss Bartlett alone in the future."

Fowle needed no second bidding.

"As for me?" inquired Carshaw, with arched eyebrows.

"May I drop you in Madison Avenue?" said Clancy. Once the police car was speeding down-town he grew chatty.

"Wish I had seen you trimming Fowle," he said pleasantly. "I've a notion he had a finger in the pie of Winifred Bartlett's dismissal."

"It may be."

Carshaw's tone was indifferent. Just then he was aware only of a very definite resentment. His mother would be waiting for dinner, and alarmed, like all mothers who own motoring sons. The detective looked surprised, but made his point, for all that.

"I suppose you'll be meeting that very charming young lady again one of these days," he said.

"I? Why? Most unlikely."

"Not so. Do you floor every man you see annoying a woman in the streets?"

"Well—er—"

"Just so. Winifred interested you. She interests me. I mean to keep an eye on her, a friendly eye. If you and she come together again, let me know."

"Really—"

THE FLIGHT 51

"No wonder you are ready with a punch. You won't let a man speak. Listen, now. The patrolman held you and Fowle because he had orders to arrest, on any pretext or none, any one who seemed to have the remotest connection with the house in One Hundred and Twelfth Street, where Winifred Bartlett lives with her aunt. You've read of the Yacht Mystery and the lassoing of Ronald Tower?"

"Mr. and Mrs. Ronald Tower are my close friends."

"Exactly. Now, Rachel Craik, Winifred's aunt, was released from custody an hour ago. She would have been charged with complicity in the supposed murder of Tower. I say 'supposed' because there was no murder. Mr. Tower has returned home, safe and sound—"

"By Jove, that's good news! But what a strange business it is! My mother was with Helen Tower this morning, trying to console her."

"Good! Now, perhaps, you'll sit up and take notice. The truth is that the mystery of this outrage on Tower is not—cannot be—of recent origin. I'm sure it is bound up with some long-forgotten occurrence, possibly a crime, in which the secret of the birth and parentage of Winifred Bartlett is involved. That girl is no more the niece of her 'aunt' than I am her nephew."

"But one is usually the niece of one's aunt."

"I think you need a cigarette," said Clancy dryly. "Organisms accustomed to poisonous stimulants often wilt when deprived too suddenly of such harmful tonics."

Carshaw edged around slightly and looked at this quaint detective.

"I apologize," he said contritely. "But the crowd got my goat when it jeered at me as a murderer. And the long wait was annoying, too."

Clancy, however, was not accustomed to having his confidences slighted. He was ruffled.

"Perhaps what I was going to say is hardly worth while," he snapped. "It was this. If, by chance, your acquaintance with Winifred Bartlett goes beyond to-day's meeting, and you learn anything of her life and history which sounds strange in your ears, you may be rendering her a far greater service than by flattening Fowle's nose if you bring your knowledge straight to the Bureau."

"I'll not forget, Mr. Clancy. But let me explain. It will be a miracle if I meet Miss Bartlett again."

"It'll be a miracle if you don't," retorted the other.

So there was a passing whiff of misunderstanding between these two, and, like every other trivial phase of a strange record, it was destined to bulk large in the imminent hazards threatening one lone girl. Thus, Clancy ceased being communicative. He might have referred guardedly to Senator Meiklejohn. But he did not. Oddly enough, his temperament was singularly alike to Carshaw's, and that is why sparks flew.

The heart, however, is deceitful, and Fate is stronger than an irritated young man whose conventional ideals have been besmirched by being marched through the streets in custody. The garage in which Carshaw's automobile was housed temporarily was located near One Hundred and Twelfth Street. He went there on the following afternoon to see the machine stripped and find out the exact extent of the damage. Yet he passed Winifred's house resolutely, without even looking at it. He returned that way at half past six, and there, on the corner, was posted Fowle—Fowle, with a swollen nose! There also was their special patrolman, with an eye for both!

The mere sight of Fowle prowling in unwholesome quest stirred up wrath in Carshaw's mind; and the heart, always subtle and self-deceiving, whispered elatedly: "Here you have an excuse for renewing an acquaintance which you wished to make yourself believe you did not care to renew."

He walked straight to the door of the brown-stone house and rang. Then he rapped. There was no answer. When he had rapped a second time he walked away, but he had not gone far when he was almost startled to find himself face to face with Winifred coming home from making some purchases, with a bag on her arm.

He lifted his hat. Winifred, with a vivid blush, hesitated and stopped. From the corner Fowle stared at the meeting, and made up his mind that it was really a rendezvous. The patrolman thought so, too, but he had new orders as to these two.

"Pardon me, Miss Bartlett," said Carshaw. "Ah, you see I know your name better than you know mine. Mine is Carshaw—Rex Carshaw, if I may introduce myself. I have this moment tapped at your door, in the hope of seeing you."

"Why so?" asked Winifred.

"Do you wish to forget the incident of yesterday evening?"

"No; hence my stopping to hear what you have to say."

"Well, then, I am here to see to the repairing of my car—not in the hope of seeing *you*, you know"—Carshaw said this with a twinkle in his eye; "though, perhaps, if the truth were known, a little in that hope, too. Then, there at the corner, I find the very man who molested you last night looking at your house, and this spurred me to knock in order to ask a favor. Was I wrong?"

"What favor, sir?"

"That, if ever you have the least cause to be displeased with the conduct of that man in the future, you will consider it as *my* business, and as an insult offered to *me*—as it will be after the trouble of last night—and that you will let me know of the matter by letter. Here is my address."

Winifred hesitated, then took the proffered card.

"But—" she faltered.

"No; promise me that. It really is my business now, you know."

"I cannot write to you. I—don't—know you."

"Then I shall only have to stand sentinel a certain number of hours every day before your house, to see that all goes well. You can't prevent me doing that, can you? The streets are free to everybody."

"You are only making fun."

"That I am not. See how stern and solemn I look. I shall stand sentinel and gaze up at your window on the chance of seeing your face. Will you show yourself sometimes to comfort me?"

"No."

"I'm sure you will."

"I'd better promise to write the letter—"

"There now, that's a point for me!"

"Oh, don't make me laugh."

"Point number two—for you have been crying, Miss Winifred!"

"I?"

"Yes, I'm sorry to say. Oh, I only wish—"

"How do you know my name?"

"What, the 'Winifred' and the 'Bartlett?' Winifred was always one of my favorite names for a girl, and you look the name all through. Well, Fowle and I were taken to the station-house last night, and in the course of the inquiry I heard your name, of course."

"Did they do anything to you for knocking down Mr. Fowle?"

"No, no. Of course, they didn't do anything to me. In fact, they seemed rather pleased. Were you anxious, then, about me?"

"I was naturally anxious, since it was I who—"

"Ah, now, don't spoil it by giving a reason. You were anxious, that is enough; let me be proud, as a recompense. And now I want to ask you two favors, one of them a great favor. The first is to tell me all you know about this Fowle. And the second—why you look so sad and have been crying. May we walk on a little way together, and then you will tell me?"

They walked on together, and for a longer time than either of them realized. Winifred was rather bewitched. Carshaw was something of a revelation to her in an elusive quality of mind or manner which she in her heart could only call "charming."

She spoke of life at Brown, Son & Brown's, in Greenwich Village. She even revealed that she had been crying because of dark clouds which had gathered round her of a sudden, doubts and fears for which she had no name, and because of a sort of dream the previous night in which she had seen a man's Indian face, and heard a hushed, grim voice say: "She must be taken out of New York—she is the image of her mother."

"Ah! And your mother—who and where is she?" asked Carshaw.

"I don't know. I can't tell. I never knew her," answered Winifred droopingly, with a shake of her head.

"And as to your father?"

"I have no father. I have only my aunt."

"Winifred," said Carshaw solemnly, "will you consider me your friend from this night?"

"You are kind. I trust you," she murmured.

"A friend is a person who acts for another with the same zeal as for himself, and who has the privilege of doing whatever seems good to him for that other. Am I to regard myself as thus privileged?"

Winifred, who had never flirted with any young man in her life, fancied she knew nothing about the rules of the game. She was confused. She veiled her eyes.

"I don't know—perhaps—we shall see," she stammered. Which was not so bad for a novice.

They parted with a warm hand-shake. Ten minutes later Carshaw was in a telephone booth with Clancy's ear at the other end of the wire.

"I have just had a chat with Miss Bartlett," he began.

"Tut, tut! How passing strange!" cackled the detective. "The merest chance in the world, I'm sure."

"Yes. The miracle came off, so you're entitled to your gibe. But I have news for you. It's about a dream and a face."

"Gee! Throw the picture on the screen, Mr. Carshaw."

Then Carshaw spoke, and Clancy listened and bade him work more miracles, even though he might have to report such phenomena to the Psychical Research Society. Next morning Carshaw, a hard man when offended, visited Brown, Son & Brown, who had executed a large rebinding order for his father's library, and Fowle was speedily out of a job. The ex-foreman knew the source of his misfortune, and vowed vengeance.

In the evening, about half past six, Carshaw was back in One Hundred and Twelfth Street. There had been no promise of a meeting between him and Winifred—no promise, but, by those roundabout means by which people in sympathy understand each other, it was perfectly well understood that they would happen to meet again that night.

He waited in the street, but Winifred did not appear. The brown-stone house was in total darkness. An hour passed, and the waiting was weary, for it was drizzling. But Carshaw waited, being a persistent young man. At last, after seven, a pang of fear shot through his breast. He remembered the girl's curious account of the dream-man.

He determined to knock at the door, relying on his wits to invent some excuse if any stranger opened. But to his repeated loud knockings there came no answer. The house seemed abandoned. Winifred was gone! Even a friendly patrolman took pity on his drawn face and drew near.

"No use, sir!" he confided. "They've skipped. But don't let on *I* told you. Call up the Detective Bureau!"

CHAPTER X
CARSHAW TAKES UP THE CHASE

"Busy, Mr. Carshaw?" inquired some one when an impatient young man got in touch with Mulberry Street after an exasperating delay.

"Not too busy to try and defeat the scoundrels who are plotting against a defenseless girl," he cried.

"Well, come down-town. We'll expect you in half an hour."

"But, Mr. Clancy asked me—"

"Better come," said the voice, and Carshaw, though fuming, bowed to authority.

It is good for the idle rich that they should be brought occasionally into sharp contact with life's realities. During his twenty-seven years Rex Carshaw had hardly ever known what it meant to have a purpose balked. Luckily for him, he was of good stock and had been well reared.

The instinct of sport, fostered by triumphs at Harvard, had developed an innate quality of self-reliance and given him a physical hardihood which revelled in conquest over difficulties. Each winter, instead of lounging in flannels at the Poinciana, he was out with guides and dogs in the Northwest after moose and caribou.

He preferred polo to tennis. He would rather pass a fortnight in oilskins with the rough and ready fisher-folk of the Maine coast than don the white ducks and smart caps of his wealthy yachting friends. In a word, society and riches had not spoiled him. But he did like to have his own way, and the suspicion that he might be thwarted in his desire to help Winifred Bartlett cut him now like a sword. So he chafed against the seeming slowness of the Subway, and fuel was added to the fire when he was kept waiting five minutes on arriving at police headquarters.

He found Clancy closeted with a big man who had just lighted a fat cigar, and this fact in itself betokened official callousness as to Winifred's fate. Hot words leaped from his lips.

"Why have you allowed Miss Bartlett to be spirited away? Is there no law in this State, nor any one who cares whether or not the law is obeyed? She's gone—taken by force. I'm certain of it."

"And we also are certain of it, Mr. Carshaw," said Steingall placidly. "Sit down. Do you smoke? You'll find these cigars in good shape," and he pushed forward a box.

"But, is nothing being done?" Nevertheless, Carshaw sat down and took a cigar. He had sufficient sense to see that bluster was useless and only meant loss of dignity.

"Sure. That's why I asked you to come along."

"You see," put in Clancy, "you short-circuited the connections the night before last, so we let you cool your heels in the rain this evening. We want no 'first I will and then I won't' helpers in this business."

Carshaw met those beady brown eyes steadily. "I deserved that," he said. "Now, perhaps, you'll forget a passing mood. I have come to like Winifred."

Clancy stared suddenly at a clock.

"Tick, tick!" he said. "Eight fifteen. *Nom d'un pipe,* now I understand."

For the first time the true explanation of Senator Meiklejohn's covert glance at the clock the previous morning had occurred to him. That wily gentleman wanted Winifred out of the house for her day's work before the police interviewed Rachel Craik. He had fought hard to gain even a few hours in the effort to hinder inquiry.

"What's bitten you, Frog?" inquired the chief.

Probably—who knows?—but there was some reasonable likelihood that the Senator's name might have reached Carshaw's ears had not the telephone bell jangled. Steingall picked up the receiver.

"Long-distance call. This is it, I guess," and his free hand enjoined silence. The talk was brief and one-sided. Steingall smiled as he replaced the instrument.

"Now, we're ready for you, Mr. Carshaw," he said, lolling back in his chair again. "The Misses Craik and Bartlett have arrived for the night at the Maples Inn, Fairfield, Connecticut. Thanks to you, we knew that some one was desperately anxious that Winifred should leave New York. Thanks to you, too, she has gone. Neither her aunt nor the other interested people cared to have her strolling in Central Park with an eligible and fairly intelligent bachelor like Mr. Rex Carshaw."

Carshaw's lips parted eagerly, but a gesture stayed him.

"Yes. Of course, I know you're straining at the leash, but please don't go off on false trails. You never lose time casting about for the true line. This is the actual position of affairs: A man known as Ralph V. Voles, assisted by an amiable person named Mick the Wolf—he was so christened in Leadville, where they sum up a tough accurately—hauled Mr. Ronald Tower into the river. For some reason best known to himself, Mr. Tower treats the matter rather as a joke, so the police can carry it no further. But Voles is associated with Rachel Craik, and was in her house during several hours on the night of the river incident and the night following. It is almost safe to assume that he counseled the girl's removal from New York because she is 'the image of her mother.' One asks why this very natural fact should render Winifred Bartlett an undesirable resident of New York. There is a ready answer. She might be recognized. Such recognition would be awkward for somebody. But the girl has lived in almost total seclusion. She is nineteen. If she is so like her mother as to be recognized, her mother must have been a person of no small consequence, a lady known to and admired by a very large circle of friends. The daughter of any other woman, presumably long since dead, who was not of social importance, could hardly be recognized. You follow this?"

"Perfectly." Carshaw was beginning to remodel his opinion of the Bureau generally, and of its easy-going, genial-looking chief in particular.

"This fear of recognition, with its certain consequences," went on Steingall, pausing to flick the ash off his cigar, "is the dominant factor in Winifred's career as directed by Rachel Craik. This woman, swayed by some lingering shreds of decent thought, had the child well educated, but the instant she approaches maturity, Winifred is set to earn a living in a bookbinding factory. Why? Social New York does not visit wholesale trade houses, nor travel on the elevated during rush hours. But it does go to the big stores and fashionable milliners where a pretty, well proportioned girl can obtain employment readily. Moreover, Rachel Craik would never 'hear of' the stage, though Winifred can sing, and believes she could dance. And how prompt recognition might be in a theater. It all comes to this, Mr. Carshaw: the Bureau's hands are tied, but it can and will assist an outsider, whom it trusts, who means rescuing Miss Bartlett from the exile which threatens her. We have looked you over carefully, and think you are trustworthy—"

"The Lord help you if you're not!" broke in Clancy. "I like the girl. It will be a bad day for the man who works her evil."

Carshaw's eyes clashed with Clancy's, as rapiers rasp in thrust and parry. From that instant the two men became firm friends, for the young millionaire said quietly:

"I have her promise to call for help on me, first, Mr. Clancy."

"You'll follow her to Fairfield then?" and Steingall sat up suddenly.

"Yes. Please advise me."

"That's the way to talk. I wish there was a heap more boys like you among the Four Hundred. But I can't advise you. I'm an official. Suppose, however, I were a young gentleman of leisure who wanted to befriend a deserving young lady in Winifred Bartlett's very peculiar circumstances. I'd persuade her to leave a highly undesirable 'aunt,' and strike out for herself. I'd ask my mother, or some other lady of good standing, to take the girl under her wing, and see that she was cared for until a place was found in some business or profession suited to her talents. And that's as far as I care to go at this sitting. As for the ways and means, in these days of fast cars and dare-devil drivers who are in daily danger of losing their licenses—"

"By gad, I'll do it," and Carshaw's emphatic fist thumped the table.

"Steady! This Voles is a tremendous fellow. In a personal encounter you would stand no chance. And he's the sort that shoots at sight. Mick the Wolf, too, is a bad man from the wild and woolly West. The type exists, even to-day. We have

CARSHAW TAKES UP THE CHASE 59

gunmen here in New York who'd clean up a whole saloonful of modern cowboys. Voles and Mick are in Fairfield, but I've a notion they'll not stay in the same hotel as Winifred and her aunt. I think, too, that they may lie low for a day or two. You'll observe, of course, that Rachel Craik, so poverty-stricken that Winifred had to earn eight dollars a week to eke out the housekeeping, can now afford to travel and live in expensive hotels. All this means that Winifred ought to be urged to break loose and come back to New York. The police will protect her if she gives them the opportunity, but the law won't let us butt in between relatives, even supposed ones, without sufficient justification. One last word—you must forget everything I've said."

"And another last word," cried Clancy. "The Bureau is a regular old woman for tittle-tattle. We listen to all sorts of gossip. Some of it is real news."

"And, by jing, I was nearly omitting one bit of scandal," said Steingall. "It seems that Mick the Wolf and a fellow named Fowle met in a corner saloon round about One Hundred and Twelfth Street the night before last. They soon grew thick as thieves, and Fowle, it appears, watched a certain young couple stroll off into the gloaming last night."

"Next time I happen on Fowle!" growled Carshaw.

"You'll leave him alone. Brains are better than brawn. Ask Clancy."

"Sure thing!" chuckled the little man. "Look at us two!"

"Anyhow, I'd hate to have the combination working against me," and with this deft rejoinder Carshaw hurried away to a garage where he was known. At dawn he was hooting an open passage along the Boston Post Road in a car which temporarily replaced his own damaged cruiser.

Within three hours he was seated in the dining-room of the Maples Inn and reading a newspaper. It was the off season, and the hotel contained hardly any guests, but he had ascertained that Winifred and her aunt were certainly there. For a long time, however, none but a couple of German waiters broke his vigil, for this thing happened before the war. One stout fellow went away. The other, a mere boy, remained and flecked dust with a napkin, wondering, no doubt, why the motorist sat hours at the table. At last, near noon, Rachel Craik, with a plaid shawl draped around her angular shoulders, and Winifred, in a new dress of French gray, came in.

Winifred started and cast down her eyes on seeing who was there. Carshaw, on his part, apparently had no eyes for her, but kept a look over the top of his newspaper at Rachel Craik, to see whether she recognized him, supposing it to be a fact that he had been seen with Winifred. She seemed, however, hardly to be aware of his presence.

The girl and the woman sat some distance from him—the room was large—near a window, looking out, and anon exchanging a remark in quiet voices. Then a lunch was brought into them, Carshaw meantime buried in the newspaper except when he stole a glance at Winifred.

His hope was that the woman would leave the girl alone, if only for one minute, for he had a note ready to slip into Winifred's hand, beseeching her to meet him that evening at seven in the lane behind the church for some talk "on a matter of high importance."

But fortune was against him. Rachel Craik, after her meal, sat again at the window, took up some knitting, and plied needles like a slow machine. The afternoon wore on. Finally, Carshaw rang to order his own late lunch, and the German boy brought it in. He rose to go to table; but, as if the mere act of rising spurred him to further action, he walked straight to Winifred. The hours left him were few, and his impatience had grown to the point of desperateness now. He bowed and held out the paper, saying:

"Perhaps you have not seen this morning's newspaper?" At the same time he presented her the note.

Miss Craik was sitting two yards away, half-turned from Winifred, but at this afternoon offer of the morning's paper she glanced round fully at Winifred, and saw, that as Winifred took the newspaper, she tried to grasp with it a note also which lay on it—tried, but failed, for the note escaped, slipped down on Winifred's lap, and lay there exposed.

Miss Craik's eyebrows lifted a little, but she did not cease her knitting. Winifred's face was painfully red, and in another moment pale. Carshaw was not often at his wits' end, but now for some seconds he stood embarrassed.

Rachel Craik, however, saved him by saying quickly: "The gentleman has dropped something in your lap, Winifred." Whereupon Winifred handed back the unfortunate note.

What was he to do now? If he wrote to Winifred through the ordinary channels of the hotel she might, indeed, soon receive the letter, but the risks of this course were many and obvious. He ate, puzzling his brains, spurring all his power of invention. The time for action was growing short.

Suddenly he noticed the German boy, and had a thought. He could speak German well, and, guessing that Rachel Craik probably did not understand a word of it, he said in a natural voice to the boy in German:

"Fond of American dollars, boy?"

"*Ja, mein Herr,*" answered the boy.

"I'm going to give you five."

"You are very good, *mein Herr,*" said the boy, "beautiful thanks!"

"But you have to earn them. Will you do just what I tell you, without asking for any reason?"

"If I can, *mein Herr.*"

"Nothing very difficult. You have only to go over yonder by that chair where I was sitting, throw yourself suddenly on the floor, and begin to kick and wriggle as though you had a fit. Keep it up for two minutes, and I will give you not five but ten. Will you do this?"

CARSHAW TAKES UP THE CHASE   61

"From the heart willingly, *mein Herr*," answered the boy, who had a solemn face and a complete lack of humor.

"Wait, then, three minutes, and then—suddenly—do it."

The three minutes passed in silence; no sound in the room, save the clicking of Carshaw's knife and fork, and the ply of Rachel Craik's knitting-needles. Then the boy lounged away to the farther end of the room; and suddenly, with a bump, he was on the floor and in the promised fit.

"Halloo!" cried Carshaw, while from both Winifred and Rachel came little cries of alarm—for a fit has the same effect as a mouse on the nerves of women.

"He's in a fit!" screamed the aunt.

"Please do something for him!" cried Winifred to Carshaw, with a face of distress. But he would not stir from his seat. The boy still kicked and writhed, lying on his face and uttering blood-curdling sounds. This was easy. He had only to make bitter plaint in the German tongue.

"Oh, aunt," said Winifred, half risen, yet hesitating for fear, "do help that poor fellow!"

Whereupon Miss Craik leaped up, caught the water-jug from the table with a rather withering look at Carshaw, and hurried toward the boy. Winifred went after her and Carshaw went after Winifred.

The older woman turned the boy over, bent down, dipped her fingers in the water, and sprinkled his forehead. Winifred stood a little behind her, bending also. Near her, too, Carshaw bent over the now quiet form of the boy.

A piece of paper touched Winifred's palm—the note again. This time her fingers closed on it and quickly stole into her pocket.

CHAPTER XI
THE TWO CARS

"It is highly improper on my part to come here and meet you," said Winifred. "What can it be that you have to say to me of such 'high importance'?"

The two were in the lane behind the church, at seven that same evening. Winifred, on some pretext, had escaped the watchful eyes of Rachel Craik, or fancied that she had, and came hurriedly to the waiting Carshaw. She was all aflutter with expectancy not untinged by fear, she knew not of what. The nights were beginning to darken early, and it was gloomy that evening, for the sky was covered with clouds and a little drizzle was falling.

"You are not to think that there is the least hint of impropriety about the matter," Carshaw assured her. "Understand, please, Winifred, that this is no lovers' meeting, but a business one, on which your whole future life depends. You cannot suppose that I have followed you to Fairfield for nothing."

"How could you possibly know that I was here?"

"From the police."

"The police *again*? What a strange thing!"

"Yes, a strange thing, and yet not so strange. They are keenly interested in you and your movements, for your good. And I, of course, still more so."

"You are wonderfully good to care. But, tell me quickly, I cannot stay ten minutes. I think my aunt suspects something. She already knows about the note dropped to-day into my lap."

"And about the boy in the fit. Does she suspect that, too?"

"What, was that a ruse? Good gracious, how artful you must be! I'm afraid of you—"

"Endlessly artful for your sake, Winifred."

"You are kind. But tell me quickly."

"Winifred, you are in danger, from which there is only one way of escape for you—namely, absolute trust in me. Pray understand that the dream in which you heard some one say, 'She must be taken away from New York' was no dream. You are here in order to be taken. This may be the first stage of a long journey. Understand also that there is no bond of duty which forces you to go against your will, for the shrewdest men in the New York police have reason to think you are not who you imagine you are, and that the woman you call your aunt is no relative of yours."

"What reason have they?" asked Winifred.

"I don't care—I don't know, they have not told me. But I believe them, and I want you to believe me. The persons who have charge of your destiny are not normal persons—more or less they have done, or are connected with wrong. There is no doubt about that. The police know it, though they cannot yet drag that wrong into the light. Do you credit what I say?"

"It is all very strange."

"It is *true*. That is the point. Have you, by the way, ever seen a man called Voles?"

"Voles? No."

"Yet that man at this moment is somewhere near you. He came in the same train with you from New York. He is always near you. He is the most intimate associate of your aunt. Think now, and tell me whether it is not a disturbing thing that you never saw this man face to face?"

"Most disturbing, if what you say is so."

"But suppose I tell you what I firmly believe—that you *have* seen him; that it was *his* face which bent over you in your half-sleep the other night, and his voice which you heard?"

"I always thought that it was no dream," said Winifred. "It was—not a nice face."

"And remember, Winifred," urged Carshaw earnestly, "that to-day and to-morrow are your last chances. You are about to be taken far away—possibly to France or England, as surely as you see those clouds. True, if you go, I shall go after you."

"You?"

"Yes, I. But, if you go, I cannot be certain how far I may be able to defend and rescue you there, as I can in America. I know nothing of foreign laws, and those who have you in their power do. On that field they may easily beat me. So now is your chance, Winifred."

"But what am I to do?" she asked in a scared tone, frightened at last by the sincerity blazing from his eyes.

"Necessity has no rules of propriety," he answered. "I have a car here. You should come with me this very night to New York. Once back there, it is only what my interest in you gives me the right to expect that you will consent to use my purse for a short while, till you find suitable employment."

Winifred covered her face and began to cry. "Oh, I couldn't!" she sobbed.

"Don't cry," said Carshaw tenderly. "You must, you know, since it is the only way. You cry because you do not trust me."

"Oh! I do. But what a thing it is that you propose! To break with all my past on a sudden. I hardly even know you; last week I had not seen you—"

"There, that is mistrust. I know you as well as if I had always known you. In fact, I always did, in a sense. Please don't cry. Say that you will come with me to-night. It will be the best piece of work that you ever did for yourself, and you will always thank me for having persuaded you."

"But not to-night! I must have time to reflect, at least."

"Then, when?"

"Perhaps to-morrow night. I don't know. I must think it over first in all its bearings. To-morrow morning I will leave a letter in the office, telling you—"

"Well, if you insist on the delay. But it is dangerous, Winifred—it is horribly dangerous!"

"I can't help that. How could a girl run away in that fashion?"

"Well, then, to-morrow night at eleven, precisely. I shall be at the end of this lane in my car, if your letter in the morning says 'Yes.' Is that understood?"

"Yes."

"Let me warn you against bringing anything with you—any clothes or a grip. Just steal out of the inn as you are. And I shall be just there at the corner—at eleven."

"Yes."

"I may not have the chance of speaking to you again before—"

But Carshaw's pleading stopped short; from the near end of the lane a tall form entered it—Rachel Craik. She had followed Winifred from the hotel, suspecting that all was not well—had followed her, lost her, and now had refound her. She walked sedately, with an inscrutable face, toward the spot where the two were talking. The moment Carshaw saw this woman of ill omen he understood that all was lost, unless he acted with bewildering promptness, and quickly he whispered in Winifred's ear:

"It must be to-night or never! Decide now. 'Yes' or 'No.'"

"Yes," said Winifred, in a voice so low that he could hardly hear.

"At eleven to-night?"

"Yes," she murmured.

Rachel Craik was now up to them. She was in a vile temper, but contrived to curb it.

"What is the meaning of this, Winifred? And who is this gentleman?" she said.

Winifred, from the habit of a lifetime, stood in no small awe of that austere woman. All the blood fled from the girl's face. She could only say brokenly:

THE TWO CARS   65

"I am coming, aunt," and went following with a dejected air a yard behind her captor. In this order they walked till they arrived at the door of the Maples Inn, neither having uttered a single word to the other. There Miss Craik halted abruptly. "Go to your room," she muttered. "I'm ashamed of you. Sneaking out at night to meet a strange man! No kitchen-wench could have behaved worse."

Winifred had no answer to that taunt. She could not explain her motives. Indeed, she would have failed lamentably had she attempted it. All she knew was that life had suddenly turned topsy-turvy. She distrusted her aunt, the woman to whom she seemed to owe duty and respect, and was inclined to trust a young man whom she had met three times in all. But she was gentle and soft-hearted. Perhaps, if this Mr. Rex Carshaw, with his earnest eyes and wheedling voice, could have a talk with "aunty," his queer suspicions—so oddly borne out by events—might be dissipated.

"I'm sorry if I seem to have done wrong," she said, laying a timid hand on Rachel Craik's arm. "If you would only tell me a little, dear. Why have we left New York? Why—"

"Do you want to see me in jail?" came the harsh whisper.

"No. Oh, no. But—"

"Obey me, then! Remain in your room till I send for you. I'm in danger, and you, you foolish girl, are actually in league with my enemies. Go!"

Winifred sped through the porch, and hied her to a window in her room on the first floor which commanded a view of the main street. She could see neither Carshaw nor Aunt Rachel, the one having determined to lie low for a few hours, and the other being hidden from sight already as she hastened through the rain to the small inn where Voles and Mick the Wolf were located.

These worthies were out. The proprietor said they had hired a car and gone to Bridgeport. Miss Craik could only wait, and she sat in the lobby, prim and quiet, the picture of resignation, not betraying by a look or gesture the passions of anger, apprehension, and impatience which raged in her breast.

Voles did not come. An hour passed; eight struck, then nine. Once the word "carousing"! passed Miss Rachel's lips with an intense bitterness; but, on the whole, she sat with a stiff back, patient as stone.

Then after ten there came the hum and whir of an automobile driven at high speed through the rain-sodden main street. It stopped outside the inn. A minute later the gallant body of Voles entered, cigar in his mouth, and a look of much champagne in his eyes.

"What, Rachel, girl, you here!" he said in his offhand way.

"Are you sober?" asked Rachel, rising quickly.

"Sober? Never been really soused in my life! What's up?"

He dropped a huge paw roughly on her shoulder, and her hard eyes softened as she looked at his face and splendid frame, for Ralph "Voles" was Rachel Craik's one weakness.

"What's the trouble?" he went on, seeing that her lips were twitching.

"You should have been here," she snapped. "Everything may be lost. A man is down here after Winifred, and I've caught her talking to him in secret."

"A cop?" and Voles glanced around the otherwise deserted lobby.

"I don't know—most probably. Or he may be that same man who was walking with her on Wednesday night in Central Park. Anyway, this afternoon he tried to hand her a note in offering her a newspaper. The note fell, and I saw it. Afterward he managed to get it to her in some way, though I never for a moment let her out of my sight; and they met about seven o'clock behind the church."

"The little cat! She beat you to it, Rachel!"

"There is no time for talk, Ralph. That man will take her from us, and then woe to you, to William, to us all. Things come out; they do, they do—the deepest secrets! Man, man—oh, rouse yourself, sober yourself, and act! We must be far from this place before morning."

"No more trains from here—"

"You could hire a car for your own amusement. Rush her off in that. Snatch her away to Boston. We may catch a liner to-morrow."

"But we can't have her seeing us!"

"We can't help that. It is dark; she won't see your face. Let us be gone. We must have been watched, or how could that man have found us out? Ralph! Don't you understand? You must do something."

"Where's this spy you gab of? I'll—"

"This is not the Mexican border. You can't shoot here. The man is not the point, but the girl. She must be gotten away at once."

"Nothing easier. Off, now to the hotel, and be ready in half an hour. I'll bring the car around."

Rachel Craik wanted no further discussion. She reached the Maples Inn in a flurry of little runs. Before the door she saw two glaring lights, the lamps of Carshaw's automobile. It was not far from eleven. Even as she approached the hotel, Carshaw got in and drove down the street. He drew up on a patch of grass by the roadside at the end of the lane behind the church. Soon after this he heard a clock strike eleven.

His eyes peered down the darkness of the lane to see Winifred coming, as she had promised. It was still drizzling slightly—the night was heavy, stagnant and silent. Winifred did not come, and Carshaw's brows puckered with care and foreboding. A quarter of an hour passed, but no light tread gladdened his ear. Fairfield lay fast asleep.

Carshaw could no longer sit still. He paced restlessly about the wet grass to ease his anxious heart. And so another quarter of an hour wore slowly. Then the sound of a fast-moving car broke the silence. Down the road a pair of dragon-eyes blazed. The car came like the chariots of Sennacherib, in reckless flight. Soon it was upon him. He drew back out of the road toward his own racer.

Though rather surprised at this urgent flight he had no suspicion that Winifred might be the cause of it. As the car dashed past he clearly saw on the front seat two men, and in the tonneau he made out the forms of two women. The faces of any of the quartet were wholly merged in speed and the night, but some white object fluttered in the swirl of air and fell forlornly in the road, dropping swiftly in its final plunge, like a stricken bird. He darted forward and picked up a lady's handkerchief. Then he knew! Winifred was being reft from him again. He leaped to his own car, started the engine, turned with reckless haste, and in a few seconds was hot in chase.

CHAPTER XII

THE PURSUIT

The two automobiles rushed along the Boston Post Road, heading for Bridgeport. The loud rivalry of their straining engines awoke many a wayside dweller, and brought down maledictions on the heads of all midnight joy-riders.

Carshaw knew the road well, and his car was slightly superior to the other in speed. His hastily evolved plan was to hold the kidnappers until they were in the main street of Bridgeport. There he could dash ahead, block further progress, risking a partial collision if necessary, and refer the instant quarrel to the police, bidding them verify his version of the dispute by telephoning New York.

He could only hope that Winifred would bear him out as against her "aunt," and he felt sure that Voles and his fellow-adventurer dare not risk close investigation by the law. At any rate, his main object at present was to overtake the car in front, which had gained a flying start, and thus spoil any maneuvering for escape, such as turning into a side road. In his enthusiasm he pressed on too rapidly.

He was seen, and his intent guessed. The leading car slowed a trifle in rounding a bend; as Carshaw careened into view a revolver-shot rang out, and a bullet drilled a neat hole in the wind-screen, making a noise like the sharp crack of a whip. Simultaneously came a scream!

That must be Winifred's cry of terror in his behalf. The sound nerved him anew. He saw red. A second shot, followed by a wilder shriek, spat lead somewhere in the bonnet. Carshaw set his teeth, gave the engine every ounce of power, and the two chariots of steel went raging, reckless of consequences, along the road.

There must be a special Providence that looks after chauffeurs, as well as after children and drunkards, for at some places the road, though wide enough, was so dismal with shadow that if any danger lurked within the darkness it would not have been seen in time to be avoided.

"Drunkenness" is, indeed, the word to describe the state of mind of the two drivers by this time—a heat to be on, a wrath against obstacles, a storm in the blood, and a light in the eyes. Voles would have whirled through a battalion of soldiers on the march, if he had met them, and would have hissed curses at them as he pitched over their bodies. He knew how to handle an automobile, having driven one over the rough tracks of the Rockies, so this well-kept road offered no difficulties. For five minutes the cars raged ahead, passed through a sleeping village street and down a hill into open country beyond.

No sound was made by their occupants, whose minds and purposes remained dark one to the other. Voles might have fancied himself chased by the flight of witches who harried Tam o' Shanter, while Carshaw might have been hunting a cargo of ghosts; only the running hum of the cars droned its music along the highway, with a staccato accompaniment of revolver-shots and Winifred's appeals to heaven for aid. Meantime, the rear car still gained on the one in front. And, on a sudden, Carshaw was aware of a shouting, though he could not make out the words. It was Mick the Wolf, who had clambered into the tonneau and was bellowing:

"Pull up, you—Pull up, or I'll get you sure!"

Nor was the threat a waste of words, for he had hardly shouted when again a bullet flicked past Carshaw's head.

Just then a bend of the road and a patch of woodland hid the two cars from each other; but they had hardly come out upon a reach of straight road again when another shot was fired. Carshaw, however, was now crouched low over the steering wheel, and using the hood of the car as a breast-work; though, since he was obliged to look out, his head was still more or less exposed.

He bated no whit of speed on this account, but raced on; still, that firing in the dark had an effect upon his nerves, making him feel rather queer and small, for every now and again at intervals of a few seconds, it was sure to come, the desperado taking slow, cool aim with the perseverance of a man plying his day's work, of a man repeating to himself the motto:

"If at first you don't succeed, try, try, try again."

Those shots, moreover, were coming from a hand whose aim seldom failed—a dead shot, baffled only by the unconquerable vibration. And yet Carshaw was untouched. He could not even think. He was conscious only of the thrum of the car, the spurts of flame, the whistle of lead, the hysterical frenzy of Winifred's plaints.

The darkness alone saved him, but the more he caught up with the fugitive the less was this advantage likely to stand him in good stead. And when he should actually catch them up—what then? This question presented itself now to his heated mind. He had no plan of action. None was possible. Even in Bridgeport what could he do? There were two against one—he would simply be shot as he passed the other car.

It was only the heat of the hunt that had created in him the feeling that he must overtake them, though he died for it; but when he was within thirty yards of the front car, and two shots had come dangerously near in swift succession, a flash of reason warned him, and he determined to slacken speed a little. He was not given time to do this. There was an outcry on the car in front from three throats in it.

A mob of oxen, being driven to some market, blocked the road just beyond a bend. The men in charge had heard the thunder of the oncoming racers, with its ominous obbligato of screams and shooting. They had striven desperately to whack the animals to the hedge on either side, and were bawling loud warnings to those thrice accursed gunmen whom they imagined chased by police. Their efforts, their yells, were useless. Sixty miles an hour demands at least sixty yards for safety. When Voles put hand and foot to the brakes he had hardly a clear space of ten. An obstreperous bullock was the immediate cause of disaster. Facing the dragon eyes, it charged valiantly!

Mick the Wolf, running short of cartridges, was about to ask Voles to slow down until he "got" the reckless pursuer, when he found himself describing a parabola backward through the air. He landed in the roadway, breaking his left arm.

Voles had an extraordinary lurid oath squeezed out of his vast bulk as he was forced onto the steering-wheel, the pillar snapping like a carrot. Winifred and Rachel Craik were flung against the padded back of the driving seat, but saved from real injury because of their crouching to avoid Mick the Wolf.

Voles was as quick as a wildcat in an emergency like this. He was on his feet in a second, with a leg over the door, meaning to shoot Carshaw ere the latter could do anything to protect himself. But luck, dead against honesty thus far, suddenly veered against crime. Carshaw's car smashed into the rear of the heavy mass composed of crushed bullock and automobile no longer mobile, and dislocated its own engine and feed pipes. The jerk threw Voles heavily, and nearly, not quite, sprained his ankle. So, during a precious second or two, he lay almost stunned on the left side of the road.

Carshaw, given a hint of disaster by the slightest fraction of time, and already braced low in the body of his car, was able to jump unobserved from the wreck. As though his brain were illumined by a flash of lightning, he remembered that the signal handkerchief had fluttered from the off side of the flying car, so he ran to the right, and grabbed a breathless bundle of soft femininity out of the ruin.

"Winifred," he gasped.

"Oh, are you safe?" came the strangled sob. So that was her first thought, his safety! It is a thrilling moment in a man's life when he learns that his well-being provides an all-sufficing content for some dear woman. Come weal, come woe, Carshaw knew then that he was clasping his future wife in his arms. He ran with her through a mob of frightened cattle, and discovered a gate leading into a field.

"Can you stand if I lift you over?" he said, leaning against the bars.

"Of course! I can run, too," and, in maidenly effort to free herself, she hugged him closer. They crossed the gate and together breasted a slight rise through scattered sheaves of corn-shucks. Meanwhile, Voles and the cattlemen were engaged in a cursing match until Rachel Craik, recovering her wind, screamed an eldrich command:

"Stop, you fool! They're getting away. He has taken her down the road!"

Voles limped off in pursuit, and Mick the Wolf took up the fierce argument with the drivers. At that instant the wreck blazed into flame. Rachel had to move quickly to avoid a holocaust in which a hapless bullock provided the burnt offering. The light of this pyre revealed the distant figures of Winifred and Carshaw, whereupon the maddened Voles tried pot shots at a hundred yards. Bullets came close, too. One cut the heel of Carshaw's shoe; another plowed a ridge through his motoring cap. Realizing that Voles would aim only at him, he told Winifred to run wide.

She caught his hand.

"Please—help!" she breathed. "I cannot run far."

He smothered a laugh of sheer joy. Winifred's legs were supple as his. She was probably the fleeter of the two. It was the mother-instinct that spoke in her. This was her man, and she must protect him, cover him from enemies with her own slim body.

Soon they were safe from even a chance shot. On climbing a rail fence, Carshaw led the girl clearly into view until a fold in the ground offered. Then they doubled and zigzagged. They saw some houses, but Carshaw wanted no explanation or parleying then and pressed on. They entered a lane, or driveway, and followed it. There came a murmuring of mighty waters, the voice of the sea; they were on the beach of Long Island Sound. Far behind, in the gloom, shone a lurid redness, marking the spot where the two cars and the bullock were being converted into ardent gasses.

Carshaw halted and surveyed a long, low line of blackness breaking into the deep-blue plain of the sea to the right.

"I know where we are," he said. "There's a hotel on that point. It's about two miles. You could walk twenty, couldn't you?"

"Oh, yes," said Winifred unthinkingly.

"Or run five at a jog-trot?" he teased her.

"Well—er—"

She blushed furiously, and thanked the night that hid her from his eyes. No maid wishes a man to think she is in love with him before he has uttered the word of love. When next she spoke, Winifred's tone was reserved, almost distant.

"Now tell me what has caused this tornado," she said. "I have been acting on impulse. Please give me some reasonable theory of to-night's madness."

It was on the tip of Carshaw's tongue to assure her that they were going to New York by the first train, and would hie themselves straight to the City Hall for a marriage license. But—he had a mother, a prized and deeply reverenced mother. Ought he to break in on her placid and well-balanced existence with the curt announcement that he was married, even to a wife like Winifred. Would he be playing the game with those good fellows in the detective bureau? Was it fair even to Winifred that she should be asked to pay the immediate price, as it were, of her rescue? So the fateful words were not uttered, and the two trudged on, talking with much common sense, probing the doubtful things in Winifred's past life, and ever avoiding the tumult of passion which must have followed their first kiss.

In due course an innkeeper was aroused and the mishap of a car explained.

The man took them for husband and wife; happily, Winifred did not overhear Carshaw's smothered:

"Not yet!"

The girl soon went to her room. They parted with a formal hand-shake; but, to still the ready lips of scandal, Carshaw discovered the landlord's favorite brand of wine and sat up all night in his company.

CHAPTER XIII

THE NEW LINK

Steingall and Clancy were highly amused by Carshaw's account of the "second burning of Fairfield," as the little man described the struggle between Winifred's abductors and her rescuer. The latter, not so well versed in his country's history as every young American ought to be, had to consult a history of the Revolution to learn that Fairfield was burned by the British in 1777. The later burning, by the way, created a pretty quarrel between two insurance companies, the proprietors of two garages and the owner of a certain bullock, with Carshaw's lawyer and a Bridgeport lawyer, instructed by "Mr. Ralph Voles," as interveners.

"And where is the young lady now?" inquired Steingall, when Carshaw's story reached its end.

"Living in rooms in a house in East Twenty-seventh Street, a quiet place kept by a Miss Goodman."

"Ah! Too soon for any planning as to the future, I suppose?"

"We talked of that in the train. Winifred has a voice, so the stage offers an immediate opening. But I don't like the notion of musical comedy, and the concert platform demands a good deal of training, since a girl starts there practically as a principal. There is no urgency. Winifred might well enjoy a fortnight's rest. I have counseled that."

"A stage wait, in fact," put in Clancy, sarcastically.

By this time Carshaw was beginning to understand the peculiar quality of the small detective's wit.

"Yes," he said, smiling into those piercing and brilliant eyes. "There are periods in a man's life when he ought to submit his desires to the acid test. Such a time has come now for me."

"But 'Aunt Rachel' may find her. Is she strong-willed enough to resist cajoling, and seek the aid of the law if force is threatened?"

"Yes, I am sure now. What she heard and saw of those two men during the mad run along the Post Road supplied good and convincing reasons why she should refuse to return to Miss Craik."

"Why are you unwilling to charge them with attempted murder?" said Steingall, for Carshaw had stipulated there should be no legal proceedings.

"My lawyers advise against it," he said simply.

"You've consulted them?"

"Yes, called in on my way here. When I reached home after seeing Winifred fixed comfortably in Miss Goodman's, I opened a letter from my lawyers, requesting an interview—on another matter, of course. Meaning to marry Winifred, if she'll take me, I thought it wise to tell them something about recent events."

Steingall carefully chose a cigar from a box of fifty, all exactly alike, nipped the end off, and lighted it. Clancy's fingers drummed impatiently on the table at which the three were seated. Evidently he expected the chief to play Sir Oracle. But the head of the Bureau contented himself with the comment that he was still interested in Winifred Bartlett's history, and would be glad to have any definite particulars which Carshaw might gather.

Clancy sighed so heavily on hearing this "departmental" utterance that Carshaw was surprised.

"If I could please myself, I'd rush Winifred to the City Hall for a marriage license to-day," he said, believing he had fathomed the other's thought.

"I'm a bit of a Celt on the French and Irish sides," snapped Clancy, "and that means an ineradicable vein of romance in my make-up. But I'm a New York policeman, too—a guy who has to mind his own business far more frequently than the public suspects."

And there the subject dropped. Truth to tell, the department had to tread warily in stalking such big game as a Senator. Carshaw was a friend of the Towers, and "the yacht mystery" had been deliberately squelched by the highly influential persons most concerned. It was impolitic, it might be disastrous, if Senator Meiklejohn's name were dragged into connection with that of the unsavory Voles on the flimsy evidence, or, rather, mere doubt, affecting Winifred Bartlett's early life.

Winifred herself lived in a passive but blissful state of dreams during the three weeks. Perhaps, in her heart of hearts, she wondered if every young man who might be in love with a girl imposed such rigid restraint on himself as Rex Carshaw when he was in her company. The unspoken language of love was plain in every glance, in every tone, in the merest touch of their hands. But he spoke no definite word, and their lips had never met.

Miss Goodman, who took an interest in the pretty and amiable girl, spent many an hour of chat with her. Every morning there arrived a present of flowers from Carshaw; every afternoon Carshaw himself appeared as regularly as the clock and drank of Miss Goodman's tea. They were weeks of *Nirvana* for Winifred, and, but for her fear of being found out and her continued lack of occupation, they were the happiest she had ever known. Meantime, however, she was living on "borrowed" money, and felt herself in a false position.

"Well, any news?" was always Carshaw's first question as he placed his hat over his stick on a chair. And Winifred might reply:

"Not much. I saw such-and-such a stage manager, and went from such an agent to another, and had my voice tried, with the usual promises. I'm afraid that even your patience will soon be worn out. I am sorry now that I thought of singing instead of something else, for there are plenty of girls who can sing much better than I."

"But don't be so eager about the matter, Winifred," he would say. "It is an anxious little heart that eats itself out and will not learn repose. Isn't it? And it chafes at being dependent on some one who is growing weary of the duty. Doesn't it?"

"No, I didn't mean that," said Winifred with a rueful and tender smile. "You are infinitely good, Rex." They had soon come to the use of Christian names. Outwardly they were just good friends, while inwardly they resembled two active volcanoes.

"Now I am 'infinitely good,' which is really more than human if you think it out," he laughed. "See how you run to extremes with nerves and things. No, you are not to care at all, Winnie. You have a more or less good voice. You know more music than is good for you, and sooner or later, since you insist on it, you will get what you want. Where is the hurry?"

"You don't or won't understand," said Winifred. "I know what I want, and must get some work without delay."

"Well, then, since it upsets you, you shall. I am not much of an authority about professional matters myself, but I know a lady who understands these things, and I'll speak to her."

"Who is this lady?" asked Winifred.

"Mrs. Ronald Tower."

"Young—nice-looking?" asked Winifred, looking down at the crochet work in her lap. She was so taken up with the purely feminine aspect of affairs that she gave slight heed to a remarkable coincidence.

"Er—so-so," said Carshaw with a smile borne of memories, which Winifred's downcast eyes just noticed under their raised lids.

"What is she like?" she went on.

"Let me see! How shall I describe her? Well, you know Gainsborough's picture of the Duchess of Devonshire? She's like that, full-busted, with preposterous hats, dashing—rather a beauty!"

"Indeed!" said Winifred coldly. "She must be awfully attractive. A *very* old friend?"

"Oh, rather! I knew her when I was eighteen, and she was *elancée* then."

"What does *elancée* mean?"

"On the loose."

"What does *that* mean?"

"Well—a bit free and easy, doesn't it? Something of that sort. Smart set, you know."

"I see. Do *you*, then, belong to the smart set?"

"I? No. I dislike it rather. But one rubs with all sorts in the grinding of the mill."

"And this Mrs. Ronald Tower, whom you knew at eighteen, how old was she then?"

"About twenty-two or so."

"And she was—gay then?"

"As far as ever society would let her."

"How—did you know?"

"I—well, weren't we almost boy and girl together?"

"I wonder you can give yourself the pains to come to spend your precious minutes with me when that sort of woman is within—"

"What, not jealous?" he cried joyously. "And of that *passée* creature? Why, she isn't worthy to stoop and tie the latchets of your shoes, as the Scripture saith!"

"Still, I'd rather not be indebted to that lady for anything," said Winifred.

"But why not? Don't be excessive, little one. There is no reason, you know."

"How does she come to know about singing and theatrical people?"

"I don't know that she does. I only assume it. A woman of the world, cutting a great dash, yet hard up—that kind knows all sorts and conditions of men. I am sure she could help you, and I'll have a try."

"But is she the wife of the Ronald Tower who was dragged by the lasso into the river?"

"The same."

"It is odd how that name keeps on occurring in my life," said Winifred musingly. "A month ago I first heard it on Riverside Drive, and since then I hear it always. I prefer, Rex, that you do not say anything to that woman about me."

"I shall!" said Rex playfully. "You mustn't start at shadows."

Winifred was silent. After a time she asked:

"Have you seen Mr. Steingall or Mr. Clancy lately?"

"Yes, a couple of days ago. We are always more or less in communication. But I have nothing to report. They're keeping track of Voles and Mick the Wolf, but those are birds who don't like salt on their tails. You know already that the Bureau never ceases to work at the mystery of your relation with your impossible 'aunt,' and I think they have information which they have not passed on to me."

"Is my aunty still searching for me, I wonder?" asked Winifred.

"Oh, don't call her aunty—call her your antipodes! It is more than that woman knows how to be your aunt. Of course, the whole crew of them are moving heaven and earth to find you! Clancy knows it. But let them try—they won't succeed. And even if they do, please don't forget that I'm here now!"

"But why should they be so terribly anxious to find me? My aunty always treated me fairly well, but in a cold sort of a way which did not betray much love. So love can't be their motive."

"Love!" And Carshaw breathed the word softly, as though it were pleasing to his ear. "No. They have some deep reason, but what that is is more than any one guesses. The same reason made them wish to take you far from New York, though what it all means is not very clear. Time, perhaps, will show."

The same night Rex Carshaw sat among a set which he had not frequented much of late—in Mrs. Tower's drawing-room. There were several tables surrounded with people of various American and foreign types playing bridge. The whole atmosphere was that of Mammon; one might have fancied oneself in the halls of a Florentine money-changer. At the same table with Carshaw were Mrs. Tower, another society dame, and Senator Meiklejohn, who ought to have been making laws at Washington.

Tower stood looking on, the most unimportant person present, and anon ran to do some bidding of his wife's. Carshaw's only relation with Helen Tower of late had been to allow himself to be cheated by her at bridge, for she did not often pay, especially if she lost to one who had been something more than a friend. When he did present himself at her house, she felt a certain gladness apart from the money which he would lose; women ever keep some fragment of the heart which the world is not permitted to scar and harden wholly.

She grew pensive, therefore, when he told her that he wished to place a girl on the concert stage, and wished to know from her how best to succeed. She thought dreamily of other days, and the slightest pin-prick of jealousy touched her, for Carshaw had suddenly become earnest in broaching this matter, and the other pair of players wondered why the game was interrupted for so trivial a cause.

"What is the girl's name?" she asked.

"Her name is of no importance, but, if you must know, it is Winifred Bartlett," he answered.

Senator Meiklejohn laid his thirteen cards face upward on the table. There had been no bidding, and his partner screamed in protest:

"Senator, what are you doing?"

He had revealed three aces and a long suit of spades.

"We must have a fresh deal," smirked Mrs. Tower.

"Well, of all the wretched luck!" sighed the other woman. Meiklejohn pleaded a sudden indisposition, yet lingered while a servant summoned Ronald Tower to play in his stead.

Carshaw knew Winifred—that same Winifred whom he and his secret intimates had sought so vainly during three long weeks! Voles and his arm-fractured henchman were recuperating in Boston, but Rachel Craik and Fowle were hunting New York high and low for sight of the girl.

Fowle, though skilled in his trade, found well-paid loafing more to his choice, for Voles had sent Rachel to Fowle, guessing this man to be of the right kidney for underhanded dealings. Moreover, he knew Winifred, and would recognize her anywhere. Fowle, therefore, suddenly blossomed into a "private detective," and had reported steady failure day after day. Rachel Craik had never ascertained Carshaw's name, as it was not necessary that he should register in the Fairfield Inn, and Fowle, with a nose still rather tender to the touch, never spoke to her of the man who had smashed it.

So these associates in evil remained at cross-purposes until Senator Meiklejohn, when the bridge game was renewed and no further information was likely to ooze out, went away from Mrs. Tower's house to nurse his sickness. He recovered speedily. A note was sent to Rachel by special messenger, and she, in turn, sought Fowle, whose mean face showed a blotchy red when he learned that Winifred could be traced by watching Carshaw.

"I'll get her now, ma'am," he chuckled. "It'll be dead easy. I can make up as a parson. Did that once before when—well, just to fool a bunch of people. No one suspects a parson—see? I'll get her—sure!"

CHAPTER XIV
A SUBTLE ATTACK

Voles was brought from Boston. Though Meiklejohn dreaded the man, conditions might arise which would call for a bold and ruthless rascality not quite practicable for a Senator.

The lapse of time, too, had lulled the politician's suspicions of the police. They seemed to have ceased prying. He ascertained, almost by chance, that Clancy was hot on the trail of a gang of counterfeiters. "The yacht mystery" had apparently become a mere memory in the Bureau.

So Voles came, with him Mick the Wolf, carrying a left arm in splints, and the Senator thought he was taking no risk in calling at the up-town hotel where the pair occupied rooms the day after Carshaw blurted out Winifred's name to Helen Tower. He meant paying another visit that day, so was attired *de rigueur*, a fact at which Voles, pipe in mouth and lounging in pajamas, promptly scoffed.

"Gee!" he cried. "Here's the Senator mooching round again, dressed up to the nines—dust coat, morning suit, boots shining, all the frills—but visiting low companions all the same. Why doesn't the man turn over a new leaf and become good?"

"Oh, hold your tongue!" said William. "We've got the girl, Ralph!"

"Got the girl, have we? Not the first girl you've said that about—is it, my wily William?"

"Listen, and drop that tone when you're speaking to me, or I'll cut you out for good and all!" said Meiklejohn in deadly earnest. "If ever you had need to be serious, it is now. I said we've got her, but that only means that we are about to get her address; and the trouble will be to get herself afterward."

"Tosh! As to that, only tell me where she is, an' I'll go and grab her by the neck."

"Don't be such a fool. This is New York and not Mexico, though you insist on confounding the two. Even if the girl were without friends, you can't go and seize people in that fashion over here, and she has at least one powerful friend, for the man who beat you hollow that night, and carried her off under your very nose, is Rex Carshaw, a determined youngster, and rich, though not so rich as he thinks he is. And there must be no failure a second time, Ralph. Remember that! Just listen to me carefully. This girl is thinking of going on the stage! Do you realize what that means, if she ever gets there? You have yourself said she is the living image of her mother. You know that her mother was well known in society. Think, then, of her appearing before the public, and of the certainty of her being recognized by some one, or by many, if she does. Fall down this time, and the game's up!"

"The thing seems to be, then, to let daylight into Carshaw," said Voles.

"Oh, listen, man! Listen! What we have to do is to place her in a lonely house—in the country—where, if she screams, her screams will not be heard; and the only possibility of bringing her there is by ruse, not by violence."

"Well, and how get her there?"

"That has to be carefully planned, and even more carefully executed. It seems to me that the mere fact of her wishing to go on the stage may be made a handle to serve our ends. If we can find a dramatic agent with whom she is in treaty, we must obtain a sheet of his office paper, and write her a letter in his name, making an appointment with her at an empty house in the country, some little distance from New York. None of the steps presents any great difficulty. In fact, all that part I undertake myself. It will be for you, your friend Mick, and Rachel Craik to receive her and keep her eternally when you once have her. You may then be able so to work upon her as to persuade her to go quietly with you to South America or England. In any case, we shall have shut her away from the world, which is our object."

"Poor stuff! How about this Carshaw? Suppose he goes with her to keep the appointment, or learns from her beforehand of it? Carshaw must be wiped out."

"He must certainly be dealt with, yes," said Meiklejohn, "but in another manner. I think—I think I see my way. Leave him to me. I want this girl out of New York State in the first instance. Suppose you go to the Oranges, in New Jersey, pick out a suitable house, and rent it? Go to-day."

Voles raised his shaggy eyebrows.

"What's the rush?" he said amusedly. "After eighteen years—"

"Will you never learn reason? Every hour, every minute, may bring disaster."

"Oh, have it your way! I'll fix Carshaw if he camps on my trail a second time."

Meiklejohn returned to his car with a care-seamed brow. He was bound now for Mrs. Carshaw's apartment.

If he was fortunate enough to find her in, and alone, he would take that first step in "dealing with" her son which he had spoken of to Voles. He made no prior appointment by phone. He meant catching her unawares, so that Rex could have no notion of his presence.

Mrs. Carshaw was a substantial lady of fifty, a society woman of the type to whom the changing seasons supply the whole duty of man and woman, and the world outside the orbit of the Four Hundred is a rumor of no importance.

She had met Senator Meiklejohn in so many places for so many years that they might be called comrades in the task of dining and making New York look elegant. She was pleased to see him. Their common fund of scandal and epigram would carry them safely over a cheerful hour.

"And as to the good old firm of Carshaw—prosperous as usual, I hope," said Meiklejohn, balancing an egg-shell tea-cup.

Mrs. Carshaw shrugged.

"I don't know much about it," she said, "but I sometimes hear talk of bad times and lack of capital. I suppose it is all right. Rex does not seem concerned."

"Ah! but the mischief may be just there," said Meiklejohn. "The rogue may be throwing it all on the shoulders of his managers, and letting things slide."

"He may—he probably is. I see very little of him, really, especially just lately."

"Is it the same little influence at work upon him as some months ago?" asked Meiklejohn, bending nearer, a real confidential crony.

"Which same little influence?" asked the lady, agog with a sense of secrecy, and genuinely anxious as to anything affecting her son.

"Why, the girl, Winifred Bartlett."

"Bartlett! As far as I know, I have never even heard her name."

"Extraordinary! Why, it's the talk of the club."

"Tell me. What is it all about?"

"Ah, I must not be indiscreet. When I mentioned her, I took it for granted that you knew all about it, or I should not have told tales out of school."

"Yes, but you and I are of a different generation than Rex. He belongs to the spring, we belong to the autumn. There is no question of telling tales out of school as between you and him. So now, please, you are going to tell me *all*."

"Well, the usual story: A girl of lower social class; a young man's head turned by her wiles; the conventions more or less defied; business yawned at; mother, friends, everything shelved for the time being, and nothing important but the one thing. It's not serious, perhaps. So long as business is not *too* much neglected, and no financial consequences follow, society thinks not a whit worse of a young man on that account—on one condition, mark you! There must be no question of marriage. But in this case there *is* that question."

"But this is merely ridiculous!" laughed Mrs. Carshaw shrilly. "Marriage! Can a son of mine be so quixotic?"

"It is commonly believed that he is about to marry her."

"But how on earth has it happened that I never heard a whisper of this preposterous thing?"

"It *is* extraordinary. Sometimes the one interested is the last to hear what every one is talking about."

"Well, I never was so—amused!" Yet Mrs. Carshaw's wintry smile was not joyous. "Rex! I must laugh him out of it, if I meet him anywhere!"

"That you will not succeed in doing, I think."

"Well, then I'll frown him out of it. This is why—I see all now."

"There you are hardly wise, to think of either laughing or frowning him out of it," said Meiklejohn, offering her worldly wisdom. "No, in such cases there is a better way, take my word for it."

"And that is?"

"Approach the girl. Avoid carefully saying one word to the young man, but approach *the girl*. That does it, if the girl is at all decent, and has any sensibility. Lay the facts plainly before her. Take her into your confidence—this flatters her. Invoke her love for the young man whom she is hurting by her intimacy with him—this puts her on her honor. Urge her to fly from him—this makes her feel herself a martyr, and turns her on the heroic tack. That is certainly what I should do if I were you, and I should do it without delay."

"You're right. I'll do it," said Mrs. Carshaw. "Do you happen to know where this girl is to be found?"

"No. I think I can tell, though, from whom you might get the address—Helen Tower. I heard your son talking to her last night about the girl. He was wanting to know whether Helen could put him in the way of placing her on the stage."

"What! Is she one of those scheming chorus-girls?"

"It appears so."

"But has he had the effrontery to mention her in this way to other ladies? It is rather amusing! Why, it used to be said that Helen Tower was his *belle amie*."

"All the more reason, perhaps, why she may be willing to give you the address, if she knows it."

"I'll see her this very afternoon."

"Then I must leave you at leisure now," said Meiklejohn sympathetically.

An hour later Mrs. Carshaw was with Helen Tower, and the name of Winifred Bartlett arose between them.

"But he did not give me her address," said Mrs. Tower. "Do you want it pressingly?"

"Why, yes. Have you not heard that there is a question of marriage?"

"Good gracious! Marriage?"

The two women laid their heads nearer together, enjoying the awfulness of the thing, though one was a mother and the other was pricked with jealousy in some secret part of her nature.

"Yes—marriage!" repeated the mother. Such an enormity was dreadful.

"It sounds too far-fetched! What will you do?"

"Senator Meiklejohn recommends me to approach the girl."

A SUBTLE ATTACK

"Well, perhaps that is the best. But how to get her address? Perhaps if I asked Rex he would tell it, without suspecting anything. On the other hand, he might take alarm."

"Couldn't you say you had secured her a place on the stage, and make him send her to you, to test her voice, or something? And then you could send her on to me," said the elder woman.

"Yes, that might be done," answered Helen Tower. "I'd like to see her, too. She must be extraordinarily pretty to capture Rex. Some of those common girls are, you know. It is a caprice of Providence. Anyway, I shall find her out, or have her here somehow within the next few days, and will let you know. First of all, I'll write Rex and ask him to come for bridge to-night."

She did this, but without effect, for Carshaw was engaged elsewhere, having taken Winifred to a theater.

However, Meiklejohn was again at the bridge party, and when he asked whether Mrs. Carshaw had paid a visit that afternoon, and the address of the girl had been given, Helen Tower answered:

"I don't know it. I am now trying to find out."

The Senator seemed to take thought.

"I hate interfering," he said at last, "but I like young Carshaw, and have known his mother many a year. It's a pity he should throw himself away on some chit of a girl, merely because she has a fetching pair of eyes or a slim ankle, or Heaven alone knows what else it is that first turns a young man's mind to a young woman. I happen to have heard, however, that Winifred Bartlett lives in a boarding-house kept by Miss Goodman in East Twenty-seventh Street. Now, my name must not—"

Helen Tower laughed in that dry way which often annoyed him.

"Surely by this time you regard me as a trustworthy person," she said.

So Fowle had proven himself a capable tracker, and Winifred's persecutors were again closing in on her. But who would have imagined that the worst and most deadly of them might be the mother of her Rex? That, surely, was something akin to steeping in poison the assassin's dagger.

CHAPTER XV
THE VISITOR

"Are you Miss Winifred Bartlett?" asked Mrs. Carshaw the next afternoon in that remote part of East Twenty-seventh Street which for the first time bore the rubber tires of her limousine.

"Yes, madam," said Winifred, who stood rather pale before that large and elegant presence. It was in the front room of the two which Winifred occupied.

"But—where have I seen you before?" asked Mrs. Carshaw suddenly, making play with a pair of mounted eye-glasses.

"I cannot say, madam. Will you be seated?"

"What a pretty girl you are!" exclaimed the visitor, wholly unconscious of the calm insolence which "society" uses to its inferiors. "I'm certain I have seen you somewhere, for your face is perfectly familiar, but for the life of me I cannot recall the occasion."

Mrs. Carshaw was not mistaken. Some dim cell of memory was stirred by the girl's likeness to her mother. For once Senator Meiklejohn's scheming had brought him to the edge of the precipice. But the dangerous moment passed. Rex's mother was thinking of other and more immediate matters. Winifred stood silent, scared, with a foreboding of the meaning of this tremendous visit.

"Now, I am come to have a quiet chat with you," said Mrs. Carshaw, "and I only hope that you will look on me as a friend, and be perfectly at your ease. I am sorry the nature of my visit is not of a quite pleasant nature, but no doubt we shall be able to understand each other, for you look good and sweet. Where have I seen you before? You are a sweetly pretty girl, do you know? I can't altogether blame poor Rex, for men are not very rational creatures, are they? Come, now, and sit quite near beside me on this chair, and let me talk to you."

Winifred came and sat, with tremulous lip, not saying a word.

"First, I wish to know something about yourself," said Mrs. Carshaw, trying honestly to adopt a motherly tone. "Do you live here all alone? Where are your parents?"

"I have none—as far as I know. Yes, I live here alone, for the present."

"But no relatives?"

THE VISITOR

"I have an aunt—a sort of aunt—but—"

"You are mysterious—'a sort of aunt.' And is this 'sort of aunt' with you here?"

"No. I used to live with her, but within the last month we have—separated."

"Is that my son's doings?"

"No—that is—no."

"So you are quite alone?"

"Yes."

"And my son comes to see you?"

"He comes—yes, he comes."

"But that is rather defiant of everything, is it not?"

A blush of almost intense carmine washed Winifred's face and neck. Mrs. Carshaw knew how to strike hard. Every woman knows how to hurt another woman.

"Miss Goodman, my landlady, usually stays in here when he comes," said she.

"All the time?"

"Most of the time."

"Well, I must not catechise you. No one woman has the right to do that to another, and you are sweet to have answered me at all. I think you are good and true; and you will therefore find it all the easier to sympathize with my motives, which have your own good at heart, as well as my son's. First of all, do you understand that my son is very much in love with you?"

"I—you should not ask me—I may have thought that he liked me. Has—he—told you so?"

"He has never mentioned your name to me. I never knew of your existence till yesterday. But it is so; he is fond of you, to such an unusual extent, that quite a scandal has arisen in his social set—"

"Not about me?"

"Yes."

"But there is nothing——"

"Yes; it is reported that he intends to marry you."

"And is that what the scandal is about? I thought the scandal was when you did not marry, not when you did."

Mrs. Carshaw permitted herself to be surprised. She had not looked for such weapons in Winifred's armory. But she was there to carry out what she deemed an almost sacred mission, and the righteous can be horribly unjust.

"Yes, in the middle classes, but not in the upper, which has its own moral code—not a strictly Biblical one, perhaps," she retorted glibly. "With us the scandal is not that you and my son are friends, but that he should seriously think of marrying you, since you are on such different levels. You see, I speak plainly."

Winifred suddenly covered her face with her hands. For the first time she measured the great gulf yawning between her and that dear hope growing up in her heart.

"That is how the matter stands before marriage," went on Mrs. Carshaw, sure that she was kind in being merciless. "You can conceive how it would be afterwards. And society is all nature—it never forgives; or, if it forgives, it may condone sins, but never an indiscretion. Nor must you think that your love would console my son for the great social loss which his connection with you threatens to bring on him. It will console him for a month, but a wife is not a world, nor, however beloved, does she compensate for the loss of the world. If, therefore, you love my son, as I take it that you do—do you?"

Winifred's face was covered. She did not answer.

"Tell me in confidence. I am a woman, too, and know—"

A sob escaped from the poor bowed head. Mrs. Carshaw was moved. She had not counted on so hard a task. She had even thought of money!

"Poor thing! That will make your duty very hard. I wish—but there is no use in wishing! Necessity knows no pity. Winifred, you must summon all your strength of mind, and get out of this false position."

"What am I to do? What can I do?" wailed Winifred. She was without means or occupation, and could not fly from the house.

"You can go away," said Mrs. Carshaw, "without letting him know whither you have gone, and till you go you can throw cold water on his passion by pretending dislike or indifference—"

"But could I do such a thing, even if I tried?" came the despairing cry.

"It will be hard, certainly, but a woman should be able to accomplish everything for the man she loves. Remember for whose sake you will be doing it, and promise me before I leave you."

"Oh, you should give me time to think before I promise anything," sobbed Winifred. "I believe I shall go mad. I am the most unfortunate girl that ever lived. I did not seek him—he sought me; and now, when I—Have you no pity?"

"You see that I have—not only pity, but confidence. It is hard, but I feel that you will rise to it. I, and you, are acting for Rex's sake, and I hope, I believe, you will do your share in saving him. And now I must go, leaving my sting behind me. I am so sorry! I never dreamed that I should like you so well. I have seen you before somewhere—it seems to me in an old dream. Good-by, good-by! It had to be done, and I have done it, but not gladly. Heaven help us women, and especially all mothers!"

Winifred could not answer. She was choked with sobs, so Mrs. Carshaw took her departure in a kind of stealthy haste. She was far more unhappy now than when she entered that quiet house. She came in bristling with resolution. She went out, seemingly victorious, but feeling small and mean.

THE VISITOR

When she was gone Winifred threw herself on a couch with buried head, and was still there an hour later when Miss Goodman brought up a letter. It was from a dramatic agent whom she had often haunted for work—or rather it was a letter on his office paper, making an appointment between her and a "manager" at some high-sounding address in East Orange, New Jersey, when, the writer said, "business might result."

She had hardly read it when Rex Carshaw's tap came to the door.

About that same time Steingall threw a note across his office table to Clancy, who was there to announce that in a house in Brooklyn a fine haul of coiners, dies, presses, and other illicit articles, human and inanimate, had just been made.

"Ralph V. Voles and his bad man from the West have come back to New York again," said the chief. "You might give 'em an eye."

"Why on earth doesn't Carshaw marry the girl?" said Clancy.

"I dunno. He's straight, isn't he?"

"Strikes me that way."

"Me, too. Anyhow, let's pick up a few threads. I've a notion that Senator Meiklejohn thinks he has side-stepped the Bureau."

Clancy laughed. His mirth was grotesque as the grin of one of those carved ivories of Japan, and to the effect of the crinkled features was added a shrill cackle. The chief glanced up.

"Don't do that," he said sharply. "You get my goat when you make that beastly noise!"

These two were beginning again to snap at each other about the Senator and his affairs, and their official quarrels usually ended badly for the other fellow.

CHAPTER XVI
WINIFRED DRIFTS

Winifred, pale as death, rose to receive her lover, with that letter in her hand which made an appointment with her at a house in East Orange; a letter which she believed to have been written by a dramatic agent, but which was actually inspired by Senator Meiklejohn. It was the bait of the trap which should put her once more in the power of Meiklejohn and his accomplices.

During a few tense seconds the girl prayed for power to play the bitter part which had been thrust upon her—to play it well for the sake of the man who loved her, and whom she loved. The words of his mother were still in her ears. She had to make him think that she did not care for him. In the last resort she had to fly from him. She had tacitly promised to do this woeful thing.

Far enough from her innocent mind was it to dream that the visit of Rex's mother had been brought about by her enemies in order to deprive her of a protector and separate her from her lover at the very time when he was most necessary to save her.

Carshaw entered in high spirits. "Well, I have news—" he began. "But, hello! What's the matter?"

"With whom?" asked Winifred.

"You look pale."

"Do I? It is nothing."

"You have been crying, surely."

"Have I?"

"Tell me. What is wrong?"

"Why should I tell *you*, if anything is wrong?"

He stood amazed at this speech. "Odd words," said he, looking at her in a stupor of surprise, almost of anger. "Whom should you tell but me?"

This touched Winifred, and, struggling with the lump in her throat, she said, unsteadily: "I am not very well to-day; if you will leave me now, and come perhaps some other time, you will oblige me."

Carshaw strode nearer and caught her shoulder.

"But what a tone to me! Have I done something wrong, I wonder? Winnie, what is it?"

"I have told you I am not very well. I do not desire your company—to-day."

"Whew! What majesty! It must be something outrageous. But what? Won't you be dear and kind, and tell me?"

"You have done nothing."

"Yes, I have. I think I can guess. I spoke of Helen Tower yesterday as of an old sweetheart—was that it? And it is all jealousy. Surely I didn't say much. What on earth did I say? That she was like a Gainsborough; that she was rather a beauty; that she was *elancée* at twenty-two. But I didn't mean any harm. Why, it's jealousy!"

At this Winifred drew herself up to discharge a thunderbolt, and though she winced at the Olympian effort, managed to say distinctly:

"There can be no jealousy where there is no love."

Carshaw stood silent, momentarily stunned, like one before whom a thunderbolt has really exploded. At last, looking at the pattern of a frayed carpet, he said humbly enough:

"Well, then, I must be a very unfortunate sort of man, Winifred."

"Don't believe me!" Winifred wished to cry out. But the words were checked on her white lips. The thought arose in her, "He that putteth his hand to the plow and looketh back—"

"It is sudden, this truth that you tell me," went on Carshaw. "Is it a truth?"

"Yes."

"You are not fond of me, Winnie?"

"I have a liking for you."

"That's all?"

"That is all."

"Don't say it, dear. I suffer."

"Do you? No, don't suffer. I—can't help myself."

"You are sorry for me, then?"

"Oh, yes."

"But how came I, then, to have the opposite impression so strongly? I think—I can't help thinking—that it was your fault, dear. You made me hope, perhaps without meaning me to, that—that life was to be happy for me. When I entered that door just now no man in New York had a lighter step than I, or a more careless heart. I shall go out of it—different, dear. You should not have allowed me to think—what I did; and you should not have told me the truth so—quite so—suddenly."

"Sit down. You are not fair to me. I did not know you cared—"

"You—you did not know that I cared? Come, that's not true, girl!"

"Not so much, I mean—not quite so much. I thought that you were flirting with me, as I—perhaps—was flirting with you."

"Who is that I hear speaking? Is it Winifred? The very sound of her voice seems different. Am I dreaming? She flirting with me? I don't realize her—it is a different girl! Oh! this thing comes to me like a falling steeple. It had no right to happen!"

"You should sit down, or you should go; better go—better, better go," and Winifred clutched wildly at her throat. "Let us part now, and let us never meet!"

"If you like, if you wish it," said Carshaw, still humbly, for he was quite dazed. "It seems sudden. I am not sure if it is a dream or not. It isn't a happy one, if it is. But have we no business to discuss before you send me away in this fashion? Do you mean to throw off my help as well as myself?"

"I shall manage. I have an offer of work here in my hands. I shall soon be at work, and will then send the amount of the debt which I owe you, though you care nothing about that, and I know that I can never repay you for all."

"Yes, that is true, too, in a way. Am I, then, actually to go?"

"Yes."

"But you are not serious? Think of my living on, days and years, and not seeing you any more. It seems a pitiable thing, too. Even you must be sorry for me."

"Yes, it seems a pitiable thing!"

"So—what do you say?"

"Good-by. Go—go!"

"But you will at least let me know where you are? Don't be quite lost to me."

"I shall be here for some time. But you won't come. I mustn't see you. I demand that much."

"No, no. I won't come, you may be sure. And you, on your part, promise that if you have need of money you will let me know? That is the least I can expect of you."

"I will; but go. I will have you in my—memory. Only go from me now, if you—love—"

"Good-by, then. I do not understand, but good-by. I am all in, Winnie; but still, good-by. God bless you—"

He kissed her hand and went. Her skin was cold to his lips, and, in a numb way, he wondered why. A moment after he had disappeared she called his name, but in an awful, hushed voice which he could not hear; and she fell at her length on the couch.

"Rex! My love! My dear love," she moaned, and yet he did not hear, for the sky had dropped on him.

There she lay a little while, yet it was not all pain with her. There is one sweetest sweet to the heart, one drop of intensest honey, sweeter to it than any wormwood is bitter, which consoled her—the consciousness of self-sacrifice, of duty done, of love lost for love's sake. Mrs. Carshaw had put the girl on what Senator Meiklejohn cynically called "the heroic tack"; and, having gone on that tack, Winifred deeply understood that there was a secret smile in it, and a surprising light. She lay catching her breath till Miss Goodman brought up the tea-tray, expecting to find the cheery Carshaw there as usual, for she had not heard him go out.

Instead, she found Winifred sobbing on the couch, for Winifred's grief was of that depth which ceases to care if it is witnessed by others. The good landlady came, therefore, and knelt by Winifred's side, put her arm about her, and began to console and question her. The consolation did no good, but the questions did. For, if one is persistently questioned, one must answer something sooner or later, and the mind's effort to answer breaks the thread of grief, and so the commonplace acts as a medicine to tragedy.

In the end Winifred was obliged to sit up and go to the table where the tea-things were. This was in itself a triumph; and her effort to secure solitude and get rid of Miss Goodman was a further help toward throwing off her mood of despair. By the time Miss Goodman was gone the storm was somewhat calmed.

During that sad evening, which she spent alone, she read once more the letter making the appointment with her at East Orange. Now, reading it a second time, she felt a twinge of doubt. Who could it be, she wondered, whom she would have to see there? East Orange was some way off. A meeting of this sort usually took place in New York, at an office.

Her mind was not at all given to suspicions, but on reading over the letter for the third time, she now noticed that the signature was not in the handwriting of the agent. She knew his writing quite well, for he had sent her other letters. This writing was, indeed, something like his, but certainly not his. It might be a clerk's; the letter was typed on his office paper.

To say that she was actually disturbed by these little rills of doubt would not be quite true. Still, they did arise in her mind, and left her not perfectly at ease. The touch of uneasiness, however, made her ask herself why she should now become a singer at all. It was Carshaw who had pressed it upon her, because she had insisted on the vital necessity of doing something quickly, and he had not wished her to work again with her hands. In reality, he was scheming to gain time.

Now that they were parted she saw no reason why she should not throw off all this stage ambition, and toil like other girls as good as she. She had done it. She was skilled in the bookbinding craft; she might do it again. She counted her money and saw that she had enough to carry her on a week, or even two, with economy. Therefore, she had time in which to seek other work.

Even if she did not find it she would have not the slightest hesitation in "borrowing" from Rex; for, after all, all that he had was hers—she knew it, and he knew it. Before she went to bed she decided to throw up the singing ambition, not to go to the appointment at East Orange, but to seek some other more modest occupation.

About that same hour Rex Carshaw walked desolately to the apartment in Madison Avenue. He threw himself into a chair and propped his head on a hand, saying: "Well, mother!" for Mrs. Carshaw was in the room.

His mother glanced anxiously at him, for though Winifred had promised to keep secret the fact of her visit, she was in fear lest some hint of it might have crept out; nor had she foreseen quite so deadly an effect on her son as was now manifest. He looked care-worn and weary, and the maternal heart throbbed.

She came and stood over him. "Rex, you don't look well," said she.

"No; perhaps I'm not very well, mother," said he listlessly.

"Can I do anything?"

"No; I'm rather afraid that the mischief is beyond you, mother."

"Poor boy! It is some trouble, I know. Perhaps it would do you good to tell me."

"No; don't worry, mother. I'd rather be left alone, there's a dear."

"Only tell me this. Is it very bad? Does it hurt—much?"

"Where's the use of talking? What cannot be cured must be endured. Life isn't all a smooth run on rubber tires."

"But it will pass, whatever it is. Bear up and be brave."

"Yes; I suppose it will pass—when I am dead."

She tried to smile.

"Only the young dream of death as a relief," she said. "But such wild words hurt, Rex."

"That's all right, only leave me alone; you can't help. Give me a kiss, and then go."

A tear wet his forehead when Mrs. Carshaw laid her lips there.

CHAPTER XVII
ALL ROADS LEAD TO EAST ORANGE

The next day Winifred set about her new purpose of finding some other occupation than that connected with the stage, though she rose from bed that morning feeling ill, having hardly slept throughout the night.

First, she read over once more the "agent's" letter, and was again conscious of an extremely vague feeling of something queer in it when she reflected on the lateness of the hour of the rendezvous—eight in the evening. She decided to write, explaining her change of purpose, and declining the interview with this nebulous "client." She did not write at once. She thought that she would wait, and see first the result of the day's search for other employment.

Soon after breakfast she went out, heading for Brown's, her old employers in Greenwich Village, who had turned her away after the yacht affair and the arrest of her aunt.

As she waited at the crossing where the cars pass, her eyes rested on a man—a clergyman, apparently—standing on the opposite pavement. He was not at the moment looking that way, and she took little notice of him, though her subconsciousness may have recognized something familiar in the lines of his body.

It was Fowle in a saintly garb, Fowle in a shovel hat, Fowle interested in the comings and goings of Winifred. Fowle, moreover, in those days, floated on the high tide of ease, and had plenty of money in his pocket. He not only looked, but felt like a person of importance, and when Winifred entered a street-car, Fowle followed in a taxi.

There was a new foreman at Brown's now, and he received the girl kindly. She laid her case before him. She had been employed there and had given satisfaction. Then, all at once, an event with which she had nothing more to do than people in China, had caused her to be dismissed. Would not the firm, now that the whole business had blown over, reinstate her?

The man heard her attentively through and said:

"Hold on. I'll have a talk with the boss." He left her, and was gone ten minutes. Then he returned, with a shaking head. "No, Brown's never take any one back," said he; "but here's a list of bookbinding firms which he's written out for you, and he says he'll give you a recommendation if any of 'em give you a job."

With this list Winifred went out, and, determined to lose no time, started on the round, taking the nearest first, one in Nineteenth Street. She walked that way, and slowly behind her followed a clergyman. The firm in Nineteenth Street wanted no new hand. Winifred got into a Twenty-third Street cross-town car. After her sped a taxi.

And now, when she stopped at the third bookbinder's, Fowle knew her motive. She was seeking work at the old trade. He was puzzled, knowing that she had wished to become a singer, and being aware, too, of the appointment for the next night at East Orange. Had she, then, changed her purpose? Perhaps she was seeking both kinds of employment, meaning to accept the one which came first. If the bookbinding won out that might be dangerous to the rendezvous.

In any case, Fowle resolved to nip the project in the bud. He would go later in the day to all the firms she had visited, ask if they had engaged her, and, if so, drop a hint that she had been dismissed from Brown's for being connected with the crime committed against Mr. Ronald Tower. A bogus clergyman's word was good for something, anyhow.

From Twenty-third Street, where there was no work, Winifred made her way to Twenty-ninth Street, followed still by the taxi. Here things turned out better for her. She was seen by a manager who told her that they would be short-handed in three or four days, and that, if she could really produce a reference from Brown's he would engage her permanently. Winifred left him her address, so that he might write and tell her when she could come.

She lunched in a cheap restaurant and walked to her lodgings. Color flooded her cheeks, but she was appalled by her loneliness, by the emptiness of her life. To bind books and to live for binding books, that was not living. She had peeped into Paradise, but the gate had been shut in her face, and the bookbinding world seemed an intolerably flat and stale rag-fair in comparison.

How was she to live it through, she asked herself. When she went up to her room the once snug and homely place disgusted her. How was she to live through the vast void of that afternoon alone in that apartment? How bridge the vast void of to-morrow? The salt had lost its savor; she tasted ashes; life was all sand of the desert; she would not see him any more. The resolution which had carried her through the interview with Carshaw failed her now, and she blamed herself for the murder of herself.

"Oh, how could I have done such a thing!" she cried, bursting into tears, with her hat still on and her head on the table.

She had to write a letter to the "agent," telling him that she did not mean to keep the rendezvous at East Orange, since she had obtained other work, and with difficulty summoned the requisite energy. Every effort was nauseous to her. Her whole nature was absorbed in digesting her one great calamity.

Next morning it was the same. Her arms hung listlessly by her side. She evaded little domestic tasks. Though her clothes were new, a girl can always find sewing and stitching. A certain shirtwaist needed slight adjustment, but her fingers fumbled a simple task. She passed the time somehow till half past four. At that hour there was a ring at the outer door. In the absorption of her grief she did not hear it, though it was "his" hour. A step sounded on the stairs, and this she heard; but she thought it was Miss Goodman bringing tea.

Then, brusquely, without any knock, the door opened, and she saw before her Carshaw.

"Oh!" she screamed, in an ecstasy of joy, and was in his arms.

The rope which bound her had snapped thus suddenly for the simple reason that Carshaw had promised never to come again, and was very strict, as she knew, in keeping his pledged word. Therefore, until the moment when her distraught eyes took in the fact of his presence, she had not the faintest hope or thought of seeing him for many a day to come, if ever.

Seeing him all at once in the midst of her desert of despair, her reason swooned, all fixed principles capsized, and instinct swept her triumphantly, as the whirlwind bears a feather, to his ready embrace. He, for his part, had broken his promise because he could not help it. He had to come—so he came. His dismissal had been too sudden to be credible, to find room in his brain. It continued to have something of the character of a dream, and he was here now to convince himself that the dream was true.

Moreover, in her manner of sending him away, in some of her words, there had been something unreal and unconvincing, with broken hints of love, even as she denied love, which haunted and puzzled his memory. If he had made a thousand promises he would still have to return to her.

"Well," said he, his face alight for joy as she moaned on his breast, "what is it all about? You unreliable little half of a nerve, Winnie!"

"I can't help it; kiss me—only once!" panted Winifred, with tears streaming down her up-turned face.

Carshaw needed no bidding. Kiss her once! Well, a man should smile.

"What is it all about?" he demanded, when Winifred was quite breathless. "Am I loved, then?"

Her forehead was on his shoulder, and she did not answer.

"It seems so," he whispered. "Silence is said to mean consent. But why, then, was I not loved the day before yesterday?"

Still Winifred dared not answer. The frenzy was passing, the moral nature re-arising, stronger than ever, claiming its own. She had promised and failed! What she did was not well for him.

"Tell me," he urged, with a lover's eagerness. "You'll have to, some time, you know."

"You promised not to come. You promised definitely," said Winifred, disengaging herself from him.

"Could I help coming?" cried he. "I was in the greatest bewilderment and misery!"

"So you will always come, even if you promise not to?"

"But I won't promise not to! Where is the need now? You love me, I love you!"

Winifred turned away from him, went to the window and looked out, seeing nothing, for the eyes of the soul were busy. Her lips were now firmly set, and during the minute that she stood there a rapid train of thought and purpose passed through her mind. She had promised to give him up, and she would go through with it. It was for him—and it was sweet, though bitter, to be a martyr. But she recognized clearly that so long as he knew where to find her the thing could never be done. She made up her mind to be gone from those lodgings by that hour the next day, and to be buried from him in some other part of the great city. She would never in that case be able to ask him for help to keep going, without giving her address, but in a few days she would have work at the new bookbinder's. This well settled in her mind, she turned inward to him, saying:

"Miss Goodman will soon bring up tea. Come, let us be happy to-day. You want to know if I love you? Well, the answer is yes, yes; so now you know, and can never doubt. I want you to stay a long time this afternoon, and I invite you to be my dear, dear guest on one condition—that you don't ask me why I told you that awful fib the day before yesterday, for I don't mean to tell you!"

Of course Carshaw took her again in his arms, and, without breaking her conditions, stayed with her till nearly six. She was sedately gay all the time, but, on kissing him good-by, she wept quietly, and as quietly she said to her landlady when he was gone:

"Miss Goodman, I am going away to-morrow—for always, I'm afraid."

Soon after this six o'clock struck. At ten minutes past the hour Miss Goodman brought up two letters.

Without looking at the handwriting on the envelopes, Winifred tore open one, laying the other on a writing-desk, this latter being from the agent in answer to the one she had written. She had told him that she did not mean to keep the appointment at East Orange, and he now assured her that he had certainly never made any appointment for her at East Orange. The thing was some blunder. New York impresarios did not make appointments in East Orange. He asked for an explanation.

Pity that she did not open this letter before the other—or the other was of a nature to drive the existence of the agent's letter—of any letter—out of her head; for days afterward that all-important message lay on the table unopened.

The note which Winifred did read was from the bookbinding manager who had all but engaged her that day. He now informed her that he would have no use for her services. The clergyman in the taxi had followed very effectively on Winifred's trail.

She was stunned by this final blow. Her eyes gazed into vacancy. What she was to do now she did not know. The next day she had to go away into strange lodgings, with hardly any money, without any possibility of her applying again to Rex, without support of any sort. She had never known real poverty, for her "aunt" had always more or less been in funds; and the prospect appalled her. She would face it, however, at all costs, and, the bookbinding failing her, her mind naturally recurred, with a gasp of hope, to the singing.

There was the appointment at East Orange at eight. She looked at the clock; she might have time, though it would mean an instant rush. She would go. True, she had written the agent to say that she would not, and he might have so advised his client. But perhaps he had not had time to do this, since she had written him so late. In any case, there was a chance that she should meet the person in question, and then she could explain. Suddenly she leaped up, hurried on her hat and coat, and ran out of the house. In a few minutes she was at the Hudson Tube, bound for Hoboken and East Orange.

Of course it was a mad thing to leave an unopened letter on the table, but just then poor Winifred was nearly out of her mind.

CHAPTER XVIII
THE CRASH

When Carshaw came, with lightsome step and heart freed from care—for in some respects he was irresponsible as any sane man could be—to visit his beloved Winifred next day, he was met by a frightened and somewhat incoherent Miss Goodman.

"Not been home all night! Surely you can offer some explanation further than that maddening statement?" cried he, when the shock of her news had sent the color from his face and the joy from his eyes.

"Oh, sir, I don't know what to say. Indeed, I am not to blame."

Miss Goodman, kind-hearted soul, was more flurried now by Carshaw's manner than by Winifred's inexplicable disappearance.

"Blame, my good woman, who is imputing blame?" he blazed at her. "But there's a hidden purpose, a convincing motive, in her going out and not returning. Give me some clue, some reason. A clear thought now, the right word from you, may save hours of useless search."

"How can I give any clues?" cried the bewildered landlady. "The dear young creature was crying all day fit to break her heart after the lady called—"

"The lady! What lady?"

"Your mother, sir. Didn't she tell you? Mrs. Carshaw was here the day before yesterday, and she must have spoken very cruelly to Winifred to make her so downcast for hours. I was that sorry for her—"

Now, Carshaw had the rare faculty—rare, that is, in men of a happy-go-lucky temperament—of becoming a human iceberg in moments of danger or difficulty. The blank absurdity of Miss Goodman's implied assertion that Winifred had run away—though, indeed, running away was uppermost in the girl's thoughts—had roused him to fiery wrath.

But the haphazard mention of his mother's visit, the coincidence of Winifred's unexpectedly strange behavior and equally unexpected transition to a wildly declared love, revealed some of the hidden sources of events, and over the volcano of his soul he imposed a layer of ice. He even smiled pleasantly as he begged Miss Goodman to dry her eyes and be seated.

"We are at loggerheads, you see," he said, almost cheerfully. "Just let us sit down and have a quiet talk. Tell me everything you know, and in the order in which things happened. Tell me facts, and if you are guessing at probabilities, tell me you are guessing. Then we shall soon unravel the tangled threads."

Thus reassured, Miss Goodman took him through the records of the past forty-eight hours, so far as she knew them. After the first few words he required no explanations of his mother's presence in that middle-class section of Manhattan. She had gone there in her stately limousine to awe and bewilder a poor little girl—to frighten an innocent out of loving her son and thus endangering her own grandiose projects for his future.

It was pardonable, perhaps, from a worldly woman's point of view. That there were other aspects of it she should soon see, with a certain definiteness, the cold outlines of which already made his mouth stern, and sent little lines to wrinkle his forehead. He had spared her hitherto—had hoped to keep on sparing her—yet she had not spared Winifred! But who had prompted her to this heartless deed? He loved his mother. Her faults were those of society, her virtues were her own. She had lived too long in an atmosphere of artificiality not to have lost much of the fine American womanliness that was her birthright. That could be cured—he alone knew how. The puzzling query, for a little while, was the identity of the cruel, calculating, ruthless enemy who struck by her hand.

There was less light shed on Winifred's own behavior. He recalled her words: "You want to know if I love you—yes, yes—I want you to stay a long time this afternoon—don't ask me why I told you that awful fib—"

And then her confession to Miss Goodman: "I am going away to-morrow—for always, I'm afraid."

What did that portend? Ah, yes; she was going to some place where he could not find her, to bury herself away from his love and because of her love for him. It was no new idea in woman's heart, this. For long ages in India sorrowing wives burned themselves to death on the funeral pyres of their lords. Poor Winifred only reversed the method of the sacrifice—its result would be the same.

"But 'to-morrow'—to-day, that is. You are quite sure of her words?" he persisted.

"Oh, yes, sir; quite sure. Besides she has left her clothes and letters, and little knick-knacks of jewelry. Would you care to see them?"

For an instant he hesitated, for he was a man of refinement, and he hated the necessity of prying into the little secrets of his dear one. Then he agreed, and Miss Goodman took him from her own sitting-room to that tenanted by Winifred. Her presence seemed to linger in the air. His eyes traveled to the chair from which she rose with that glad crooning cry when he came to her so few hours earlier.

On the table lay her tiny writing-case. In it, unopened, and hidden by the discouraging missive from the bookbinder's, rested the note from the dramatic agent, with the thrice-important clue of its plain statement: "I have made no appointment for you at any house near East Orange."

But Miss Goodman had already thrown open the door which led to Winifred's bedroom.

"You can see for yourself, sir," she said, "the room was not occupied last night. Nor that she could be in the house without me knowing it, poor thing. There are her clothes in the wardrobe, and the dressing-table is tidy. She's extraordinarily neat in her ways, is Miss Bartlett—quite different from the empty-headed creatures girls mostly are nowadays."

Miss Goodman spoke bitterly. She was fifty, gray-haired, and a hopeless old maid. This point of view sours the appearance of saucy eighteen with the sun shining in its tresses.

Carshaw swallowed something in his throat. The sanctity of this inner room of Winifred's overwhelmed him. He turned away hastily.

"All right, Miss Goodman," he said; "we can learn nothing here. Let us go back to your apartment, and I'll tell you what I want you to do now."

Passing the writing-desk again he looked more carefully at its contents. A small packet of bills caught his eye. There were the receipts for such simple articles as Winifred had bought with his money. Somehow, the mere act of examining such a list struck him with a sense of profanation. He could not do it.

His eyes glazed. Hardly knowing what the words meant, he glanced through the typed document from the bookbinder. It was obviously a business letter. He committed no breach of the etiquette governing private correspondence by reading it. So great was his delicacy in this respect that he did not even lift the letter from the table, but noted the address and the curt phraseology. Here, then, was a little explanation. He would inquire at that place.

"I want you to telegraph me each morning and evening," he said to the landlady. "Don't depend on the phone. If you have news, of course you will give it, but if nothing happens say that there is no news. Here is my address and a five-dollar bill for expenses. Did Miss Bartlett owe you anything?"

"No, sir. She paid me yesterday when she gave me notice."

"Ah! Kindly retain her rooms. I don't wish any other person to occupy them."

"Do you think, sir, she will not come back to-day?"

"I fear so. She is detained by force. She has been misled by some one. I am going now to find out who that some one else is."

He drove his car, now rejuvenated, with the preoccupied gaze of one who seeks to pierce a dark and troubled future. From the garage he called up the Long Island estate where his hacks and polo ponies were housed for the winter. He gave some instructions which caused the man in charge to blink with astonishment.

"Selling everything, Mr. Carshaw!" he said. "D'ye really mean it?"

"Does my voice sound as if I were joking, Bates?"

"No-no, sir; I can't say it does. But—"

THE CRASH

"Start on the catalogue now, this evening. I'll look after you. Mr. Van Hofen wants a good man. Stir yourself, and that place is yours."

He found his mother at home. She glanced at him as he entered her boudoir. She saw, with her ready tact, that questions as to his state of worry would be useless.

"Will you be dining at home, Rex?" she asked.

"Yes. And you?"

"I—have almost promised to dine *en famille* with the Towers."

"Better stop here. We have a lot of things to arrange."

"Arrange! What sort of things?"

"Business affairs for the most part."

"Oh, business! Any discussion of—"

"I said nothing about discussion, mother. For some years past I have been rather careless in my ways. Now I am going to stop all that. A good business maxim is to always choose the word that expresses one's meaning exactly."

"Rex, you speak queerly."

"That shows I'm doing well. Your ears have so long been accustomed to falsity, mother, that the truth sounds strangely."

"My son, do not be so bitter with me. I have never in my life had other than the best of motives in any thought or action that concerned you."

He looked at her intently. He read in her words an admission and a defense.

"Let us avoid tragedy, mother, at least in words. Who sent you to Winifred?"

"Then she has told you?"

"She has not told me. Women are either angels or fiends. This harmless little angel has been driven out of her Paradise in the hope that her butterfly wings may be soiled by the rain and mud of Manhattan. Who sent you to her?"

"Senator Meiklejohn," said Mrs. Carshaw defiantly.

"What, that smug Pharisee! What was his excuse?"

"He said you were the talk of the clubs—that Helen Tower—"

"She, too! Thank you. I see the drift of things now. It was heartless of you, mother. Did not Winifred's angel face, twisted into misery by your lies, cause you one pang of remorse?"

Mrs. Carshaw rose unsteadily. Her face was ghastly in its whiteness.

"Rex, spare me, for Heaven's sake!" she faltered. "I did it for the best. I have suffered more than you know."

"I am glad to hear it. You have a good nature in its depths, but the canker of society has almost destroyed it. That is why you and I are about to talk business."

"I am feeling faint. Let matters rest a few hours."

He strode to the bell and summoned a servant. "Bring some brandy and two glasses," he said when the man came.

It was an unusual order at that hour. Silently the servant obeyed. Carshaw looked out of the window, while his mother, true to her caste, affected nonchalance before the domestic.

"Now," said he when they were alone, "drink this. It will steady your nerves."

She was frightened at last. Her hand shook as it took the proffered glass.

"What has happened?" she asked, with quavering voice. She had never seen her son like this before. There was a hint of inflexible purpose in him that terrified her. When he spoke the new crispness in his voice shocked her ears.

"Mere business, I assure you. Not another word about Winifred. I shall find her, sooner or later, and we shall be married then, at once. But, by queer chance, I have been looking into affairs of late. The manager of our Massachusetts mills tells me that trade is slack. We have been running at a loss for some years. Our machinery is antiquated, and we have not the accumulated reserves to replace it. We are in debt, and our credit begins to be shaky. Think of that, mother—the name of Carshaw pondered over by bank managers and discounters of trade bills!"

"Senator Meiklejohn mentioned this vaguely," she admitted.

"Dear me! What an interest he takes in us! I wonder why? But, as a financial magnate, he understands things."

"Your father always said, Rex, that trade had its cycles—fat years and lean years, you know."

"Yes. He built up our prosperity by hard work, by spending less than half what he earned, not by living in a town house and gadding about in society. Do you remember, mother, how he used to laugh at your pretty little affectations? I think I own my share of the family brains, though, so I shall act now as he would have acted."

"Do you wish to goad me into hysteria? What are you driving at?" she shrieked.

"That is the way to reach the heart of the mystery—get at the facts, eh? They're simple. The business needs three hundred thousand dollars to give it solidity and staying power; then four or five years' good and economical management will set it right. We have been living at the rate of fifty thousand dollars a year. For some time we have been executing small mortgages to obtain this annual income, expecting the business to clear them. Now the estates must come to the help of the business."

"In what way?" she gasped.

"They must be mortgaged up to the hilt to pay off the small sums and find the large one. It will take ten years of nursing to relieve them of the burden. Not a penny must come from the mills."

"How shall we live?" she demanded.

"I have arranged that. Your marriage settlement of two thousand five hundred

THE CRASH   103

dollars a year is secured; that is all. How big it seemed in your eyes when you were a bride! How little now, though your real needs are less! I shall take a sufficient salary as assistant manager while I learn the business. It means two thousand dollars a year for housekeeping, and I have calculated that the sale of all our goods will pay our personal debts and leave you and me five thousand each to set up small establishments."

Mrs. Carshaw flounced into a chair. "You must be quite mad!" she cried.

"No, mother, sane—quite sane—for the first time. Don't you believe me? Go to your lawyers; the scheme is really theirs. They are good business men, and congratulated me on taking a wise step. So you see, mother, I really cannot afford a fashionable wife."

"I am—choking!" she gasped. For the moment anger filled her soul.

"Now, be reasonable, there's a good soul. Five thousand in the bank, twenty-five hundred a year to live on. Why, when you get used to it you will say you were never so happy. What about dinner? Shall we start economizing at once? Let's pay off half a dozen servants before we sit down to a chop! Eh, tears! Well, they'll help. Sometimes they're good for women. Send for me when you are calmer!"

With a look of real pity in his eyes he bent and kissed her forehead. She would have kept him with her, but he went away.

"No," he said, "no discussion, you remember; and I must fix a whole heap of things before we dine!"

CHAPTER XIX
CLANCY EXPLAINS

Carshaw phoned the Bureau, asking for Clancy or the chief. Both were out.

"Mr. Steingall will be here to-morrow," said the official in charge. "Mr. Clancy asked me to tell you, if you rang up, that he would be away till Monday next."

This was Wednesday evening. Carshaw felt that fate was using him ill, for Clancy was the one man with whom he wanted to commune in that hour of agony. He dined with his mother. She, deeming him crazy after a severe attack of calf-love, humored his mood. She was calm now, believing that a visit to the lawyers next day, and her own influence with the mill-manager and the estate superintendent, would soon put a different aspect on affairs.

A telegram came late: "No news."

He sought Senator Meiklejohn at his apartment, but the fox, scenting hounds, had broken covert.

"The Senator will be in Washington next week," said the discreet Phillips. "At present, sir, he is not in town."

Carshaw made no further inquiry; he knew it was useless. In the morning another telegram: "No news!"

He set his teeth, and smilingly agreed to accompany his mother to the lawyers'. She came away in tears. Those serious men strongly approved of her son's project.

"Rex has all his father's grit," said the senior partner. "In a little time you will be convinced that he is acting rightly."

"I shall be dead!" she snapped.

The lawyer lifted his hands with a deprecating smile. "You have no secrets from me, Mrs. Carshaw," he said. "You are ten years my junior, and insurance actuaries give women longer lives than men when they have attained a certain age."

Carshaw visited Helen Tower. She was fluttered. By note he had asked for a tête-à-tête interview. But his first words undeceived her.

"Where is Meiklejohn?" he asked.

"Do you mean Senator Meiklejohn?" she corrected him.

"Yes; the man who acted in collusion with you in kidnapping my intended wife."

"How dare you—"

"Sit down, Helen; no heroics, please. Or perhaps you would prefer that Ronald should be present?"

"This tone, Rex—to me!" She was crimson with surprise.

"You are right: it is better that Tower should not be here. He might get a worse *douche* than his plunge into the river. Now, about Meiklejohn? Why did he conspire with you and my mother to carry off Winifred Bartlett?"

"I—don't know."

"Surely there was some motive?"

"You are speaking in enigmas. I heard of the girl from you. I have never seen her. If your mother interfered, it was for your good."

He smiled cynically. The cold, far-away look in his eyes was bitter to her soul, yet he had never looked so handsome, so distinguished, as in this moment when he was ruthlessly telling her that another woman absorbed him utterly.

"What hold has Meiklejohn over you?" he went on.

She simulated tears. "You have no right to address me in that manner," she protested.

"There is a guilty bond somewhere, and I shall find it out," he said coldly. "My mother was your catspaw. You, Helen, may have been spiteful, but Meiklejohn—that sleek and smug politician—I cannot understand him. The story went that owing to an accidental likeness to Meiklejohn your husband was nearly killed. His assailant was a man named Voles. Voles was an associate of Rachel Craik, the woman who poses as Winifred's aunt. That is the line of inquiry. Do you know anything about it?"

"Not a syllable."

"Then I must appeal to Ronald."

"Do so. He is as much in the dark as I am."

"I fancy you are speaking the truth, Helen."

"Is it manly to come here and insult me?"

"Was it womanly to place these hounds on the track of my poor Winifred? I shall spare no one, Helen. Be warned in time. If you can help me, do so. I may have pity on my friends, I shall have none for my enemies."

He was gone. Mrs. Tower, biting her lips and clenching her hands in sheer rage, rushed to an escritoire and unlocked it. A letter lay there, a letter from Meiklejohn. It was dated from the Marlborough-Blenheim Hotel, Atlantic City.

"Dear Mrs. Tower," it ran, "the Costa Rica cotton concession is almost secure. The President will sign it any day now. But secrecy is more than ever important.

Tell none but Jacob. The market must be kept in the dark. He can begin operations quietly. The shares should be at par within a week, and at five in a month. Wire me the one word 'settled' when Jacob says he is ready."

"At five in a month!"

Mrs. Tower was promised ten thousand of those shares. Their nominal value was one dollar. To-day they stood at a few cents. Fifty thousand dollars! What a relief it would be! Threatening dressmakers, impudent racing agents asking for unpaid bets, sneering friends who held her I. O. U.'s for bridge losses, and spoke of asking her husband to settle; all these paid triumphantly, and plenty in hand to battle in the whirlpool for years—it was a stake worth fighting for.

And Meiklejohn? As the price of his help in gaining a concession granted by a new competitor among the cotton-producing States, he would be given five shares to her one. Why did he dread this girl? That was a fruitful affair to probe. But he must be warned. Her lost lover might be troublesome at a critical stage in the affairs of the cotton market.

She wrote a telegram: "Settled, but await letter." In the letter she gave him some details—not all—of Carshaw's visit. No woman will ever reveal that she has been discarded by a man whom she boasted was tied to her hat-strings.

Carshaw sought the detective bureau, but Steingall was away now, as well as Clancy. "You'll be hearing from one of them" was the enigmatic message he was given.

Eating his heart out in misery, he arranged his affairs, received those two daily telegrams from Miss Goodman with their dreadful words, "No news," and haunted the bookbinder's, and Meiklejohn's door hoping to see some of the crew of Winifred's persecutors. At the bookbinder's he learned of the visit of the supposed clergyman, whose name, however, did not appear in the lists of any denomination.

At last arrived a telegram from Burlington, Vermont. "Come and see me. Clancy." Grown wary by experience, Carshaw ascertained first that Clancy was really at Burlington. Then he instructed Miss Goodman to telegraph to him in the north, and quitted New York by the night train.

In the sporting columns of an evening paper he read of the sale of his polo ponies. The scribe regretted the suggested disappearance from the game of "one of the best Number Ones" he had ever seen. The Long Island estate was let already, and Mrs. Carshaw would leave her expensive flat when the lease expired.

Early next day he was greeted by Clancy.

"Glad to see you, Mr. Carshaw," said the little man. "Been here before? No? Charming town. None of the infernal racket of New York about life in Burlington. Any one who got bitten by that bug here would be afflicted like the Gadarene swine and rush into Lake Champlain. Walk to the hotel? It's a fine morning, and you'll get some bully views of the Adirondacks as you climb the hill."

"Winifred is gone. Hasn't the Bureau kept you informed?"

Clancy sighed.

"I've had Winifred on my mind for days," he said irritably. "Can't you forget her for half an hour?"

"She's gone, I tell you. Spirited away the very day I asked her to marry me."

"Well, well. Why didn't you ask her sooner?"

"I had to arrange my affairs. I am poor now. How could I marry Winifred under false pretenses?"

"What, then? Did she love you for your supposed wealth?"

"Mr. Clancy, I am tortured. Why have you brought me here?"

"To stop you from playing Meiklejohn's game. I hear that you camp outside his apartment-house. You and I are going back to New York this very day, and the Bureau will soon find your Winifred. By the way, how did you happen onto the Senator's connection with the affair?"

Taking hope, Carshaw told his story. Clancy listened while they breakfasted. Then he unfolded a record of local events.

"The Bureau has known for some time that Senator Meiklejohn's past offered some rather remarkable problems," he said, dropping his bantering air and speaking seriously. "We have never ceased making guarded inquiries. I am here now for that very purpose. Some thirty years ago, on the death of his father, he and his brother, Ralph Vane Meiklejohn, inherited an old-established banking business in Vermont. Ralph was a bit of a rake, but local opinion regarded William as a steady-going, domesticated man who would uphold the family traditions. There was no ink on the blotter during upward of ten years, and William was already a candidate for Congress when Ralph was involved in a scandal which caused some talk at the time. The name of a governess in a local house was associated with his, and her name was Bartlett."

Carshaw glanced at the detective with a quick uneasiness, which Clancy pretended not to notice.

"I have no proof, but absolutely no doubt," he continued, "that this woman is now known as Rachel Craik. She fell into Ralph Meiklejohn's clutches then, and has remained his slave ever since. Two years later there was a terrific sensation here. A man named Marchbanks was found lying dead in a lakeside quarry, having fallen or been thrown into it. This quarry was situated near the Meiklejohn house. Mrs. Marchbanks, a ward of Meiklejohn's father, died in childbirth as the result of shock when she heard of her husband's death, and inquiry showed that all her money had been swallowed up in loans to her husband for Stock Exchange speculation. Mrs Marchbanks was a noted beauty, and her fortune was estimated at nearly half a million dollars. It was all the more amazing that her husband should have lost such a great sum in reckless gambling, seeing that those who remember him say he was a nice-mannered gentleman of the old type, devoted to his wife, and with a passion for cultivating orchids. Again, why should Mrs. Marchbanks's bankers and guardians allow her to be ruined by a thoughtless fool?"

Clancy seemed to be asking himself these questions; but Carshaw, so far from

New York, and with a mind ever dwelling on Winifred, said impatiently:

"You didn't bring me here to tell me about some long-forgotten mystery?"

"Ah, quit that hair-trigger business!" snapped Clancy. "You just listen, an' maybe you'll hear something interesting. Ralph Vane Meiklejohn left Vermont soon afterward. Twelve years ago a certain Ralph Voles was sentenced to five years in a penitentiary for swindling. Mrs. Marchbanks's child lived. It was a girl, and baptized as Winifred. She was looked after as a matter of charity by William Meiklejohn, and entrusted to the care of Miss Bartlett, the ex-governess."

Carshaw was certainly "interested" now.

"Winifred! My Winifred!" he cried, grasping the detective's shoulder in his excitement.

"Tut, tut!" grinned Clancy. "Guess the story's beginning to grip. Yes. Winifred is 'the image of her mother,' said Voles. She must be 'taken away from New York.' Why? Why did this same Ralph vanish from Vermont after her father's death 'by accident'? Why does a wealthy and influential Senator join in the plot against her, invoking the aid of your mother and of Mrs. Tower? These are questions to be asked, but not yet. First, you must get back your Winifred, Carshaw, and take care that you keep her when you get her."

"But how? Tell me how to find her!" came the fierce demand.

"If you jump at me like that I'll make you stop here another week," said Clancy. "Man alive, I hate humbug as much as any man; but don't you see that the Bureau must make sure of its case before it acts? We can't go before a judge until we have better evidence than the vague hearsay of twenty years ago. But, for goodness' sake, next time you grab Winifred, rush her to the nearest clergyman and make her Mrs. Carshaw, Jr. That'll help a lot. Leave me to get the Senator and the rest of the bunch. Now, if you'll be good, I'll show you the house where your Winifred was born!"

CHAPTER XX
IN THE TOILS

East Orange seemed to be a long way from New York when Winifred hastened to the appointment at "Gateway House," traveling thither by way of the Tube and the Lackawanna Railway.

More and more did it seem strange that a theatrical agent should fix on such a rendezvous, until a plausible reason suggested itself: possibly, some noted impresario had chosen this secluded retreat, and the agent had arranged a meeting there between his client and the great man whose Olympian nod gave success or failure to aspirants for the stage.

The letter itself was reassuringly explicit as to the route she should follow.

"On leaving the station," it said, "turn to the right and walk a mile along the only road that presents itself until you see, on the left, a large green gate bearing the name 'Gateway House.' Walk in. The house itself is hidden by trees, and stands in spacious grounds. If you follow these directions, you will have no need to ask the way."

The description of the place betokened that it was of some local importance, and hope revived somewhat in her sorrowing heart at the impression that perhaps, after all, it was better she had failed in finding work at the bindery.

Notwithstanding the charming simplicity of her nature, Winifred would not be a woman if she did not know she was good-looking. The stage offered a career; work in the factory only yielded existence. Recent events had added a certain strength of character to her sweet face; and Miss Goodman, who happened to be an expert dressmaker, had used the girl's leisure in her lodgings to turn her nimble fingers to account. Hence, Winifred was dressed with neat elegance, and the touch of winter keenness in the air gave her a splendid color as she hurried out of the station many minutes late for her appointment.

Would she be asked to sing, she wondered? She had no music with her, and had never touched a piano since her music-master's anxiety to train her voice had been so suddenly frustrated by Rachel Craik. But she knew many of the solos from "Faust," "Rigoletto," and "Carmen"; surely, among musical people, there would be some appreciation of her skill if tested by this class of composition, as compared with the latest rag-time melody or gushing cabaret ballad.

Busy with such thoughts, she hastened along the road, until she awoke with a start to the knowledge that she was opposite Gateway House. Certainly the retreat was admirable from the point of view of a man surfeited with life on the Great White Way. Indeed, it looked very like a private lunatic asylum or home for inebriates, with its lofty walls studded with broken glass, and its solid gate crowned with iron spikes.

Winifred tried the door. It opened readily. She was surprised that so pretentious an abode had no lodge-keeper's cottage. There were signs of few vehicles passing over the weed-grown gravel drive, and such marks as existed were quite recent.

She was so late, however, that her confused mind did not trouble about these things, and she sped on gracefully, soon coming in full view of the house itself. It was now almost dark, and the grounds seemed very lonely; but the presence of lights in the secluded mansion gave earnest of some one awaiting her there. She fancied she heard a noise, like the snapping of a latch or lock behind her. She turned her head, but saw no one. Fowle, hiding among the evergreens, had run with nimble feet and sardonic smile to bolt the gate as soon as she was out of sight.

And now Winifred was at the front door, timidly pulling a bell. A man strolled with a marked limp around the house from a conservatory. He was a tall, strongly built person, and something in the dimly seen outline sent a thrill of apprehension through her.

But the door opened.

"I have come—" she began.

The words died away in sheer affright. Glowering at her, with a queer look of gratified menace, was Rachel Craik!

"So I see," was the grim retort. "Come in, Winnie, by all means. Where have you been all these weeks?"

"There is some mistake," she faltered, white with sudden terror and nameless suspicions. "My agent told me to come here—"

"Quite right. Be quick, or you'll miss the last train home," growled the voice of Voles behind her.

Roughly, though not violently, he pushed her inside, and the door closed.

He snapped at Rachel: "She'd be yelling for help in another second, and you never know who may be passing."

Now, Winifred was not of the order of women who faint in the presence of danger. Her love had given her a great strength; her suffering had deepened her fine nature; and her very soul rebelled against the cruel subterfuge which had been practised to separate her from her lover. She saw, with the magic intuition of her sex, that the very essence of a deep-laid plot was that Rex and she should be kept apart.

The visit of Mrs. Carshaw, then, was only a part of the same determined scheme? Rex's mother had been a puppet in the hands of those who carried her to Connecticut, who strove so determinedly to take her away when Carshaw put in an appearance, and who had tricked her into keeping this bogus appointment. She would defy them, face death itself rather than yield.

In the America of to-day, nothing short of desperate crime could long keep her from Rex's arms. What a weak, silly, romantic girl she had been not to trust in him absolutely! The knowledge nerved her to a fine scorn.

"What right have you to treat me in this way?" she cried vehemently. "You have lied to me; brought me here by a forged letter. Let me go instantly, and perhaps my just indignation may not lead me to tell my agent how you have dared to use his name with false pretense."

"Ho, ho!" sang out Voles. "The little bird pipes an angry note. Be pacified, my sweet linnet. You were getting into bad company. It was the duty of your relatives to rescue you."

"My relatives! Who are they who claim kinship? I see here one who posed as my aunt for many years—"

"Posed, Winnie?"

Miss Craik affected a croak of regretful protest.

Winifred's eyes shot lightnings.

"Yes. I am sure you are not my aunt. Many things I can recall prove it to me. Why do you never mention my father and mother? What wrong have I done to any living soul that, ever since you were mixed up in the attack on Mr. Ronald Tower, you should deal with me as if I were a criminal or a lunatic, and seek to part me from those who would befriend me?"

"Hush, little girl," interposed Voles, with mock severity. "You don't know what you're saying. You are hurting your dear aunt's feelings. She is your aunt. I ought to know, considering that you are my daughter!"

"Your daughter!"

Now, indeed, she felt ready to dare dragons. This coarse, brutal giant of a man her father! Her gorge rose at the suggestion. Almost fiercely she resolved to hold her own against these persecutors who scrupled not to use any lying device that would suit their purpose.

"Yes," he cried truculently. "Don't I come up to your expectations?"

"If you are my father," she said, with a strange self-possession that came to her aid in this trying moment, "where is my mother?"

"Sorry to say she died long since."

"Did you murder her as you tried to murder Mr. Tower?"

The chance shot went home, though it hit her callous hearer in a way she could not then appreciate. He swore violently.

"You're my daughter, I tell you," he vociferated, "and the first thing you have to learn is obedience. Your head has been turned, young lady, by your pretty Rex and his nice ways. I'll have to teach you not to address me in that fashion. Take her to her room, Rachel."

Driven to frenzy by a dreadful and wholly unexpected predicament, Winifred cast off the hand her "aunt" laid on her shoulder.

"Let me go!" she screamed. "I will not accompany you. I do not believe a word you say. If you touch me, I shall defend myself."

"Spit-fire, eh?" she heard Voles say. There was something of a struggle. She never knew exactly what happened. She found herself clasped in his giant arms and heard his half jesting protest:

"Now, my butterfly, don't beat your little wings so furiously, or you'll hurt yourself."

He carried her, screaming, up-stairs, and pushed her into a large room. Rachel Craik followed, with set face and angry words.

"Ungrateful girl!" was her cry. "After all I've done for you!"

"You stole me from my mother," sobbed Winifred despairingly. "I am sure you did. You are afraid now lest some one should recognize me. I am 'the image of my mother' that horrible man said, and I am to be taken away because I resemble her. It is you who are frightened, not I. I defy you. Even Mrs. Carshaw knew my face. I scorn you, I say, and if you think your devices can deceive me or keep Rex from me, you are mistaken. Before it is too late, let me go!"

Rachel Craik was, indeed, alarmed by the girl's hysterical outpouring. But Winifred's taunts worked harm in one way. They revealed most surely that the danger dreaded by both Voles and Meiklejohn did truly exist. From that instant Rachel Craik, who felt beneath her rough exterior some real tenderness for the girl she had reared, became her implacable foe.

"You had better calm yourself," she said quietly. "If you care to eat, food will soon be brought for you and Mr. Grey. He is your fellow-boarder for a few days!"

Then Winifred saw, for the first time, that the spacious room held another occupant. Reclining in a big chair, and scowling at her, was Mick the Wolf, whose arm Carshaw had broken recently.

"Yes," growled that worthy, "I'm not the most cheerful company, missy, but my other arm is strong enough to put that fellow of yours out o' gear if he butts in on me ag'in. So just cool your pretty lil head, will you? I'm boss here, and if you rile me it'll be sort o' awkward for you."

How Winifred passed the next few hours she could scarcely remember afterward. She noted, in dull agony, that the windows of the sitting-room she shared with Mick the Wolf were barred with iron. So, too, was the window of her bedroom. The key and handle of the bedroom lock had been taken away. Rachel Craik was her jailer, a maimed scoundrel her companion and assistant-warder.

But, when the first paroxysms of helpless pain and rage had passed, her faith returned. She prayed long and earnestly, and help was vouchsafed. Appeal to her captors was vain, she knew, so she sought the consolation that is never denied to all who are afflicted.

Neither Rachel Craik, nor the sullen bandit, nor the loud-voiced rascal who had dared to say he was her father, could understand the cheerful patience with which she met them next day.

"She's a puzzle," said Voles in the privacy of the apartment beneath. "I must dope out some way of fixin' things. She'll never come to heel again, Rachel. That fool Carshaw has turned her head."

He tramped to and fro impatiently. His ankle had not yet forgotten the wrench it received on the Boston Post Road. Suddenly he banged a huge fist on a sideboard.

"Gee!" he cried, "that should turn the trick! I'll marry her off to Fowle. If it wasn't for other considerations I'd be almost tempted—"

He paused. Even his fierce spirit quailed at the venom that gleamed from Rachel Craik's eyes.

CHAPTER XXI
MOTHER AND SON

A telegram reached Carshaw before he left Burlington with Clancy. He hoped it contained news of Winifred, but it was of a nature that imposed one more difficulty in his path.

"Not later than the twentieth," wired the manager of the Carshaw Mills in Massachusetts. Carshaw himself had inquired the latest date on which he would be expected to start work.

The offer was his own, and he could not in honor begin the new era by breaking his pledge. The day was Saturday, November 11. On the following Monday week he must begin to learn the rudiments of cotton-spinning.

"What's up?" demanded Clancy, eying the telegram, for Carshaw's face had hardened at the thought that, perhaps, in the limited time at his disposal his quest might fail. He passed the typed slip to the detective.

"Meaning?" said the latter, after a quick glance.

Carshaw explained. "I'll find her," he added, with a catch of the breath. "I must find her. God in Heaven, man, I'll go mad if I don't!"

"Cut out the stage stuff," said Clancy. "By this day week the Bureau will find a bunch of girls who're not lost yet—only planning it."

Touched by the misery in Carshaw's eyes, he added:

"What you really want is a marriage license. The minute you set eyes on Winifred rush her to the City Hall."

"Once we meet we'll not part again," came the earnest vow. Somehow, the pert little man's overweening egotism was soothing, and Carshaw allowed his mind to dwell on the happiness of holding Winifred in his arms once more rather than the uncertain prospect of attaining such bliss.

Indeed, he was almost surprised by the ardor of his love for her. When he could see her each day, and amuse himself by playing at the pretense that she was to earn her own living, there was a definite satisfaction in the thought that soon they would be married, when all this pleasant make-believe would vanish. But now that she was lost to him, and probably enduring no common misery, the complacency of life had suddenly given place to a fierce longing for a glimpse of her, for the sound of her voice, for the shy glance of her beautiful eyes.

"Now, let's play ball," said Clancy when they were in a train speeding south. "Has any complete search of Winifred's rooms been made?"

"How do you mean?"

"Did you look in every hole and corner for a torn envelope, a twisted scrap of paper, a car transfer, any mortal thing that might reveal why she went out and did not return?"

"I told you of the bookbinder's note—"

"You sure did," broke in Clancy. "You also went to the bookbinder s'teen times. Are you certain there was nothing else?"

"No—I didn't like—how could I peer and pry—"

"You'd make a bum detective. Imagine that poor girl crying her eyes out in a cold dark cell all because you were too squeamish to give her belongings the once over!"

Carshaw was not misled by Clancy's manner. He knew that his friend was only consumed by impatience to be on the trail.

"You've fired plenty of questions at me," he said quietly. "Now it's my turn. I understand why you came to Burlington, but where is Steingall all this time?"

"That big stiff! How do I know?"

In a word, Clancy was uncommunicative during a whole hour. When the mood passed he spoke of other things, but, although it was ten at night when they reached New York, he raced Carshaw straight to East Twenty-seventh Street and Miss Goodman.

There, in a few seconds, he was reading the agent's genuine note to Winifred—that containing the assurance that no appointment had been made for "East Orange."

The letter concluded:

"At first I assumed that a message intended for some other correspondent had been sent to me by error. Now, on reperusal, I am almost convinced that you wrote me under some misapprehension. Will you kindly explain how it arose?"

Clancy, great as ever on such occasions, refrained from saying: "I told you so."

"We'll call up the agent Monday, just for the sake of thoroughness," he said. "Meanwhile, be ready to come with me to East Orange to-morrow at 8 A.M."

"Why not to-night?" urged Carshaw, afire with a rage to be up and doing.

"What? To sleep there? Young man, you don't know East Orange. Run away home to your ma!"

"Where have you been?" inquired Mrs. Carshaw when her son entered. Her air was subdued. She had suffered a good deal these later days.

"To Vermont."

"Still pursuing that girl?"

"Yes, mother."

"Have you found her?"

"No, mother."

"Rex, have you driven me wholly from your heart?"

"No; that would be impossible. Winifred would not wish it, callous as you were to her."

"Do not be too hard on me. I am sore wounded. It is a great deal for a woman to be cast into the outer darkness."

"Nonsense, mother, you are emerging into light. If your friends are so ready to drop you because you are poor—with the exceeding poverty of twenty-five hundred a year—of what value were they as friends? When you know Winifred you will be glad. You will feel as Dante felt when he emerged from the Inferno."

"So you are determined to marry her?"

"Unquestionably. And mark you, mother, when the clouds pass, and we are rich again, you will be proud of your daughter-in-law. She will bear all your skill in dressing. Gad! how the women of your set will envy her complexion."

Mrs. Carshaw smiled wanly at that. She knew her "set," as Rex termed the Four Hundred.

"Why is she called Bartlett?" she inquired after a pause, and Rex looked at her in surprise. "I have a reason," she continued. "Is that her real name?"

"Now," he cried, "I admit you are showing some of your wonted cleverness."

"Ah! Then I am right. I have been thinking. Cessation from society duties is at least restful. Last night, lying awake and wondering where you were, my thoughts reverted to that girl. I remembered her face. All at once a long-forgotten chord of memory hummed its note. Twenty years ago, when you were a little boy, Rex, I met a Mrs. Marchbanks. She was a sweet singer. Does your Winifred sing?"

Carshaw drew his chair closer to his mother and placed an arm around her shoulder.

"Yes," he said.

"Rex," she murmured brokenly, hiding her face, "do you forgive me?"

"Mother, I ask you to forgive me if I said harsh things."

There was silence for a while. Then she raised her eyes. They were wet, but smiling.

"This Mrs. Marchbanks," she went on bravely, "had your Winifred's face. She was wealthy and altogether charming. Her husband, too, was a gentleman. She was a ward of the elder Meiklejohn, the present Senator's father. My recollection of events is vague, but there was some scandal in Burlington."

"I know all, or nearly all, about it. That is why I was called to Vermont. Mother, in future, you will work with me, not against me?"

"I will—indeed I will," she sobbed.

"Then you must not drop your car. I have money to pay for that. Keep in with Helen Tower, and find out what hold she has on Meiklejohn. You are good at that, you know. You understand your quarry. You will be worth twenty detectives. First, discover where Meiklejohn is. He has bolted, or shut himself up."

"You must trust me fully, or I shall not see the pitfalls. Tell me everything."

He obeyed. Before he had ended, Mrs. Carshaw was weeping again, but this time it was out of sympathy with Winifred. Next morning, although it was Sunday, her smart limousine took her to the Tower's house. Mrs. Tower was at home.

"I have heard dreadful things about you, Sarah," she purred. "What on earth is the matter? Why have you given up your place on Long Island?"

"A whim of Rex's, my dear. He is still infatuated over that girl."

"She must have played her cards well."

"Yes, indeed. One does not look for such skill in the lower orders. And how she deceived me! I went to see her, and she promised better behavior. Now I find she has gone again, and Rex will not tell me where she is. Do you know?"

"I? The creature never enters my mind."

"Of course not. She does not interest you, but I am the boy's mother, and you cannot imagine, Helen, how this affair worries me."

"My poor Sarah! It is too bad."

"Such a misfortune could not have happened had his father lived. We women are of no use where a headstrong man is concerned. I am thinking of consulting Senator Meiklejohn. He is discreet and experienced."

"But he is not in town."

"What a calamity! Do tell me where I can find him."

"I have reason to know that Rex would not brook any interference from him."

"Oh, no, of course not. It would never do to permit his influence to appear. I was thinking that the Senator might act with the girl, this wonderful Winifred. He might frighten her, or bribe her, or something of the sort."

Now, Helen Tower was not in Meiklejohn's confidence. He was compelled to trust her in the matter of the Costa Rica concession, but he was far too wise to let her into any secret where Winifred was concerned. Anxious to stab with another's hand, she thought that Mrs. Carshaw might be used to punish her wayward son.

"I'm not sure—" She paused doubtfully. "I do happen to know Mr. Meiklejohn's whereabouts, but it is most important he should not be troubled."

"Helen, you used to like Rex more than a little. With an effort, I can save him still."

"But he may suspect you, have you watched, your movements tracked."

Mrs. Carshaw laughed. "My dear, he is far too much taken up with his Winifred."

"Has he found her, then?"

"Does he not see her daily?"

Here were cross purposes. Mrs. Tower was puzzled.

"If I tell you where the Senator is, you are sure Rex will not follow you?"

"Quite certain."

"His address is the Marlborough-Blenheim, Atlantic City."

"Helen, you're a dear! I shall go there to-morrow, if necessary. But it will be best to write him first."

"Don't say I told you."

"Above all things, Helen, I am discreet."

"I fear he cannot do much. Your son is so wilful."

"Don't you understand? Rex is quite unmanageable. I depend wholly on the girl—and Senator Meiklejohn is just the man to deal with her."

They kissed farewell—alas, those Judas kisses of women! Both were satisfied, each believing she had hoodwinked the other. Mrs. Carshaw returned to her flat to await her son's arrival. If the trail at East Orange proved difficult he promised to be home for dinner.

"There will be a row if Rex meets Meiklejohn," she communed. "Helen will be furious with me. What do I care? I have won back my son's love. I have not many years to live. What else have I to work for if not for his happiness?"

So one woman in New York that night was fairly well *content*. There may be, as the Chinese proverb has it, thirty-six different kinds of mothers-in-law, but there is only one mother.

CHAPTER XXII
THE HUNT

Steingall, not Clancy, presented his bulk at Carshaw's apartment next morning. He contrived to have a few minutes' private talk with Mrs. Carshaw while her son was dressing. Early as it was, he lighted a second cigar as he stepped into the automobile, for Carshaw thought it an economy to retain a car.

"Surprised to see me?" he began. "Well, it's this way. We may drop in for a rough-house to-day. Between them, Voles and 'Mick the Wolf,' own three sound legs and three strong arms. I can't risk Clancy. He's too precious. He kicked like a mule, of course, but I made it an order."

"What of the local police?" said Carshaw.

"Nix on the cops," laughed the chief. "You share the popular delusion that a policeman can arrest any one at sight. He can do nothing of the sort, unless he and his superior officers care to face a whacking demand for damages. And what charge can we bring against Voles and company? Winifred bolted of her own accord. We must tread lightly, Mr. Carshaw. Really, I shouldn't be here at all. I came only to help, to put you on the right trail, to see that Winifred is not detained by force if she wishes to accompany you. Do you get me?"

"I believe there is good authority for the statement that the law is an ass," grumbled the other.

"Not the law. Personal liberty has to be safeguarded by the law. Millions of men have died to uphold that principle. Remember, too, that I may have to explain in court why I did so-and-so. Strange as it may sound, I've been taught wisdom by legal adversity. Now, let's talk of the business in hand. It's an odd thing, but people who wish to do evil deeds often select secluded country places to live in. I don't mind betting a box of cigars that 'East Orange' means a quiet, old-fashioned locality where there isn't a crime once in a generation."

"Some spot one would never suspect, eh?"

"Yes, in a sense. But if ever I set up as a crook—which is unlikely, as my pension is due in eighteen months—I'll live in a Broadway flat."

"I thought the city police kept a very close eye on evil-doers."

"Yes, when we know them. But your real expert is not known; once held he's done for. Of course he tries again, but he is a marked man—he has lost his confidence. Nevertheless, he will always try to be with the crowd. There is safety in numbers."

"Do you mean that East Orange is a place favorable to our search?"

"Of course it is. The police, the letter-carriers, and the storekeepers, know everybody. They can tell us at once of several hundred people who certainly had nothing to do with the abduction of a young lady. There will remain a few dozens who might possibly be concerned in such an affair. Inquiry will soon whittle them down to three or four individuals. What a different job it would be if we had to search a New York precinct, which, I take it, is about as populous as East Orange."

This was a new point of view to Carshaw, and it cheered him proportionately. He stepped on the gas, and a traffic policeman at Forty-second Street and Seventh Avenue cocked an eye at him.

"Steady," laughed Steingall. "It would be a sad blow for mother if we were held for furious driving. These blessed machines jump from twelve to forty miles an hour before you can wink twice."

Carshaw abated his ardor. Nevertheless, they were in East Orange forty minutes after crossing the ferry.

Unhappily, from that hour, the pace slackened. Gateway House had been rented from a New York agent for "Mr. and Mrs. Forest," Westerners who wished to reside in New Jersey a year or so.

Its occupants had driven thither from New York. Rachel Craik, heavily veiled and quietly attired, did her shopping in the nearest suburb, and had choice of more than one line of rail. So East Orange knew them not, nor had it even seen them.

In nowise discouraged, the man from the Bureau set about his inquiry methodically. He interviewed policemen, railway officials, postmen, and cabmen. Although the day was Sunday, he tracked men to their homes and led them to talk. Empty houses, recently let houses, houses tenanted by people who were "not particular" as to their means of getting a living, divided his attention with persons who answered to the description of Voles, Fowle, Rachel, or even the broken-armed Mick the Wolf; while he plied every man with a minutely accurate picture of Winifred.

Hither and thither darted the motor till East Orange was scoured and noted, and among twenty habitations jotted in the detective's notebook the name of Gateway House figured. It was slow work, this task of elimination, but they persisted, meeting rebuff after rebuff, especially in the one or two instances where a couple of sharp-looking strangers in a car were distinctly not welcome. They had luncheon at a local hotel, and, by idle chance, were not pleased by the way in which the meal was served.

So, when hungry again, and perhaps a trifle dispirited as the day waned to darkness with no result, they went to another inn to procure a meal. This time they were better looked after. Instead of a jaded German waiter they were served by the landlord's daughter, a neat, befrilled young damsel, who cheered them by her smile; though, to be candid, she was anxious to get out for a walk with her young man.

"Have you traveled far?" she asked, by way of talk while laying the table.

"From New York," said Steingall.

"At this hour—in a car?"

"Yes. Is that a remarkable thing here?"

"Not the car; but people in motors either whizz through of a morning going away down the coast, or whizz back again of an evening returning to New York."

"Ah!" put in Carshaw, "here is a pretty head which holds brains. It goes in for ratiocinative reasoning. Now, I'll be bound to say that this pretty head, which thinks, can help us."

A good deal of this was lost on the girl, but she caught the compliment and smiled.

"It all depends on what you want to know," she said.

"I really want to find a private prison of some sort," he said. "The sort of place where a nice-looking young lady like you might be kept in against her will by nasty, ill-disposed people."

"There is only one house of that kind in the town, and that is out of it, as an Irishman might say."

"And where is it?"

"It's called Gateway House—about a mile along the road from the depot."

Steingall, inclined at first to doubt the expediency of gossip with the girl, now pricked up his ears.

"Who lives in Gateway House?" he asked.

"No one that I know of at the moment," she answered. "It used to belong to a mad doctor. I don't mean a doctor who was mad, but— —"

"No matter about his sanity. Is he dead?"

"No, in prison. There was a trial two years ago."

"Oh! I remember the affair. A patient was beaten to death. So the house is empty?"

"It is, unless some one has rented it recently. I was taken through the place months ago. The rooms are all right, and it has beautiful grounds, but the windows frightened me. They were closely barred with iron, and the doors were covered with locks and chains. There were some old beds there, too, with straps on them. Oh, I quite shivered!"

"After we have eaten will you let us drive you in that direction in my car?" said Carshaw.

She simpered and blushed slightly. "I've an appointment with a friend," she admitted, wondering whether the swain would protest too strongly if she accepted the invitation.

"Bring him also," said Carshaw. "I assume it's a 'he.'"

"Oh, that'll be all right!" she cried.

So in the deepening gloom the automobile flared with fierce eyes along the quiet road to Gateway House, and in its seat of honor sat the hotel maid and her young man.

"That is the place," she said, after the, to her, all too brief run.

"Is this the only entrance?" demanded the chief, as he stepped out to try the gate.

"Yes. The high wall runs right round the property. It's quite a big place."

"Locked!" he announced. "Probably empty, too."

He tried squinting through the keyhole to catch a gleam of interior light.

"No use in doin' that," announced the young man. "The house stands way back, an' is hidden by trees."

"I mean having a look at it, wall or no wall," insisted Carshaw.

"But the gate is spiked and the wall covered with broken glass," said the girl.

"Such obstacles can be surmounted by ladders and folded tarpaulins, or even thick overcoats," observed Steingall.

"I'm a plumber," said the East Orange man. "If you care to run back to my place, I c'n give you a telescope ladder and a tarpaulin. But perhaps we may butt into trouble?"

"For shame, Jim! I thought you'd do a little thing like that to help a girl in distress."

"First I've heard of any girl."

"My name is Carshaw," came the prompt assurance. "Here's my card; read it by the lamp there. I'll guarantee you against consequences, pay any damages, and reward you if our search yields results."

"Jim—" commenced the girl reproachfully, but he stayed her with a squeeze.

"Cut it out, Polly," he said. "You don't wish me to start housebreaking, do you? But if there's a lady to be helped, an' Mr. Carshaw says it's O.K., I'm on. A fellow who was with Funston in the Philippines won't sidestep a little job of that sort."

Polly, appeased and delighted with the adventure, giggled. "I'd think not, indeed."

"It is lawbreaking, but I am inclined to back you up," confided Steingall to Carshaw when the car was humming back to East Orange. "At the worst you can only be charged with trespass, as my evidence will be taken that you had no unlawful intent."

THE HUNT

"Won't you come with me?"

"Better not. You see, I am only helping you. You have an excuse; I, as an official, have none—if a row springs up and doors have to be kicked open, for instance. Moreover, this is the State of New Jersey and outside my bailiwick."

"Perhaps the joker behind us may be useful."

"He will be, or his girl will know the reason why. He may have fought in every battle in the Spanish War, but she has more pep in her."

The soldierly plumber was as good as his word. He produced the ladder and the tarpaulin, and a steel wrench as well.

"If you do a thing at all do it thoroughly. That's what Funston taught us," he grinned.

Carshaw thanked him, and in a few minutes they were again looking at the tall gate and the dark masses of the garden trees silhouetted against the sky. They had not encountered many wayfarers during their three journeys. The presence of a car at the entrance to such a pretentious place would not attract attention, and the scaling of the wall was only a matter of half a minute.

"No use in raising the dust by knocking. Go over," counseled Steingall. "Try to open the gate. Then you can return the ladder and tarpaulin at once. Otherwise, leave them in position. If satisfied that the house is inhabited by those with whom you have no concern, come away unnoticed, if possible."

Carshaw climbed the ladder, sat on the tarpaulin, and dropped the ladder on the inner side of the wall. They heard him shaking the gate. His head reappeared over the wall.

"Locked," he said, "and the key gone. I'll come back and report quickly."

Jim, who had been nudged earnestly several times by his companion, cried quickly:

"Isn't your friend goin' along, too, mister?"

"No. I may as well tell you that I am a detective," put in Steingall.

"Gee whizz! Why didn't you cough it up earlier? Hol' on, there! Lower that ladder. I'm with you."

"Good old U. S. Army!" said Steingall, and Polly glowed with pride.

Jim climbed rapidly to Carshaw's side, the latter being astride the wall. Then they vanished.

For a long time the two in the car listened intently. A couple of cyclists passed, and a small boy, prowling about, took an interest in the car, but was sternly warned off by Steingall. At last they caught the faint but easily discerned sound of heavy blows and broken woodwork.

"Things are happening," cried Steingall. "I wish I had gone with them."

"Oh, I hope my Jim won't get hurt," said Polly, somewhat pale now.

They heard more furious blows and the crash of glass.

"Confound it!" growled Steingall. "Why didn't I go?"

"If I stood on the back of the car against the gate, and you climbed onto my shoulders, you might manage to stand between the spikes and jump down," cried Polly desperately.

"Great Scott, but you're the right sort of girl. The wall is too high, but the gate is possible. I'll try it," he answered.

With difficulty, having only slight knowledge of heavy cars, he backed the machine against the gate. Then the girl caught the top with her hands, standing on the back cushions.

Steingall was no light weight for her soft shoulders, but she uttered no word until she heard him drop heavily on the gravel drive within.

"Thank goodness!" she whispered. "There are three of them now. I only wish I was there, too!"

CHAPTER XXIII

"HE WHO FIGHTS AND RUNS AWAY—"

"I don't like the proposition, an' that's a fact," muttered Fowle, lifting a glass of whisky and glancing furtively at Voles, when the domineering eyes of the superior scoundrel were averted for a moment.

"Whether you like it or not, you've got to lump it," was the ready answer.

"I don't see that. I agreed to help you up to a certain point— —"

Voles swung around at him furiously, as a mastiff might turn on a wretched mongrel.

"Say, listen! If I'm up to the neck in this business, you're in it over your ears. You can't duck now, you white-livered cur! The cops know you. They had you in their hands once, and warned you to leave this girl alone. If I stand in the dock you'll stand there, too, and I'm not the man to say the word that'll save you."

"But she's with her aunt. She's under age. Her aunt is her legal guardian. I know a bit about the law, you see. This notion of yours is a bird of another color. Sham weddings are no joke. It will mean ten years."

"Who wants you to go in for a sham wedding, you swab?"

"You do, or I haven't got the hang of things."

Voles looked as though he would like to hammer his argument into Fowle with his fists. He forebore. There was too much at stake to allow a sudden access of bad temper to defeat his ends.

He was tired of vagabondage. It was true, as he told his brother long before, that he hungered for the flesh-pots of Egypt, for the life and ease and gayety of New York. An unexpected vista had opened up before him. When he came back to the East his intention was to squeeze funds out of Meiklejohn wherewith to plunge again into the outer wilderness. Now events had conspired to give him some chance of earning a fortune quickly, had not the irony of fate raised the winsome face and figure of Winifred as a bogey from the grave to bar his path.

So he choked back his wrath, and shoved the decanter of spirits across the table to his morose companion. They were sitting in the hall of Gateway House, about the hour that Carshaw and the detective, tired by their weary hunt through East Orange, sought the inn.

"Now look here, Fowle," he said, "don't be a poor dub, and don't kick at my way of speaking. *Por Dios!* man, I've lived too long in the sage country to scrape my tongue to a smooth spiel like my—my friend, the Senator. Let's look squarely at the facts. You admire the girl?"

"Who wouldn't? A pippin, every inch of her."

"You're broke?"

"Well—er—"

"You were fired from your last job. You're in wrong with the police. You adopted a disguise and told lies about Winifred to those who would employ her. What chance have you of getting back into your trade, even if you'd be satisfied with it after having lived like a plute for weeks?"

"That goes," said Fowle, waving his pipe.

"You'd like to hand one to that fellow Carshaw?"

"Wouldn't I!"

"Yet you kick like a steer when I offer you the girl, a soft, well-paid job, and the worst revenge you can take on Carshaw."

"Yes, all damn fine. But the risk—the infernal risk!"

"That's where I don't agree with you. You go away with her and her father—"

"Father! You're not her father!"

"You should be the first to believe it. Her aunt will swear it to you or to any judge in the country. Once out of the United States, she will be only too glad to avail herself of the protection matrimony is supposed to offer. What are you afraid of?"

"You talked of puttin' up some guy to pretend to marry us."

"Forget it. We can't keep her insensible or dumb for days. But, in the company of her loving father and her devoted husband, what can she do? Who will believe her? Depend on me to have the right sort of boys on the ship. They'll just grin at her. By the time she reaches Costa Rica she'll be howling for a missionary to come aboard in order to satisfy her scruples. You can suggest it yourself."

"I believe she'd die sooner."

"What matter? You only lose a pretty wife. There's lots more of the same sort when your wad is thick enough. Why, man, it means a three-months' trip and a fortune for life, however things turn out. You're tossing against luck with an eagle on both sides of the quarter."

Fowle hesitated. The other suppressed a smile. He knew his man.

"Don't decide in a minute," he said seriously. "But, once settled, there must be no shirking. Make up your mind either to go straight ahead by my orders or clear out to-night. I'll give you a ten-spot to begin life again. After that don't come near me."

"HE WHO FIGHTS AND RUNS AWAY—" 127

"I'll do it," said Fowle, and they shook hands on their compact.

It was not in Winifred's nature to remain long in a state of active resentment with any human being. A prisoner, watched diligently during the day, locked into her room at night, she met Rachel Craik's grim espionage and Mick the Wolf's evil temper with an equable cheerfulness that exasperated the one while mollifying the other.

She wondered greatly what they meant to do with her. It was impossible to believe that in the State of New Jersey, within a few miles of New York, they could keep her indefinitely in close confinement. She knew that her Rex would move heaven and earth to rescue her. She knew that the authorities, in the person of Mr. Steingall, would take up the hunt with unwearying diligence, and she reasoned, acutely enough, that a plot which embraced in its scope so many different individuals could not long defy the efforts made to elucidate it.

How thankful she was now that she had at last written and posted that long-deferred letter to the agent. Here, surely, was a clue to be followed—she had quite forgotten, in the first whirlwind of her distress, the second letter which reached her in the Twenty-seventh Street lodgings, but pinned her faith to the fact that her own note concerning the appointment "near East Orange" was in existence.

Perhaps her sweetheart was already rushing over every road in the place and making exhaustive inquiries about her. It was possible that he had passed Gateway House more than once. He might have seen amid the trees the tall chimneys of the very jail against whose iron bars her spirit was fluttering in fearful hope. Oh, why was she not endowed with that power she had read of, whose fortunate possessors could leap time and space in their astral subconsciousness and make known their thoughts and wishes to those dear to them?

She even smiled at the conceit that a true wireless telegraphy did exist between Carshaw and herself. Daily, nightly, she thought of him and he of her. But their alphabet was lacking; they could utter only the thrilling language of love, which is not bound by such earthly things as signs and symbols.

Yet was she utterly confident, and her demeanor rendered Rachel Craik more and more suspicious. Since the girl had scornfully disowned her kinship, the elder woman had not made further protest on that score. She frankly behaved as a wardress in a prison, and Winifred as frankly accepted the rôle of prisoner. There remained Mick the Wolf. Under the circumstances, no doctor or professional nurse could be brought to attend his injured arm. The broken limb had of course been properly set after the accident, but it required skilled dressing daily, and this Winifred undertook. She had no real knowledge of the subject, but her willingness to help, joined to the instruction given by the man himself, achieved her object.

It was well-nigh impossible for this rough, callous rogue, brought in contact with such a girl for the first time in his life, to resist her influence. She did not know it, but gradually she was winning him to her side. He swore at her as the cause of his suffering, yet found himself regretting even the passive part he was taking in her imprisonment.

On the very Sunday evening that Voles and Fowle were concocting their vile and mysterious scheme, Mick the Wolf, their trusted associate, partner of Voles in many a desperate enterprise in other lands, was sitting in an armchair up-stairs listening to Winifred reading from a book she had found in her bedroom. It was some simple story of love and adventure, and certainly its author had never dreamed that his exciting situations would be perused under conditions as dramatic as any pictured in the novel.

"It's a queer thing," said the man after a pause, when Winifred stopped to light a lamp, "but nobody pipin' us just now 'ud think we was what we are."

She laughed at the involved sentence. "I don't think you are half so bad as you think you are, Mr. Grey," she said softly. "For my part, I am happy in the belief that my friends will not desert me."

"Lookut here," he said with gruff sympathy, "why don't you pull with your people instead of ag'in' 'em. I know what I'm talkin' about. This yer Voles—but, steady! Mebbe I best shut up."

Winifred's heart bounded. If this man would speak he might tell her something of great value to her lover and Mr. Steingall when they came to reckon up accounts with her persecutors.

"Anything you tell me, Mr. Grey, shall not be repeated," she said.

He glanced toward the door. She understood his thought. Rachel Craik was preparing their evening meal. She might enter the room at any moment, and it was not advisable that she should suspect them of amicable relations. Assuredly, up to that hour, Mick the Wolf's manner admitted of no doubt on the point. He had been intractable as the animal which supplied his oddly appropriate nickname.

"It's this way," he went on in a lower tone. "Voles an' Meiklejohn are brothers born. Meiklejohn, bein' a Senator, an' well in with some of the top-notchers, has a cotton concession in Costa Rica which means a pile of money. Voles is cute as a pet fox. He winded the turkey, an' has forced his brother to make him manager, with a whackin' salary and an interest. I'm in on the deal, too. Bless your little heart, you just stan' pat, an' you kin make a dress outer dollar bills."

"But what have I to do with all this? Why cannot you settle your business without pursuing me?" was the mournful question, for Winifred never guessed how greatly the man's information affected her.

"I can't rightly say, but you're either with us or ag'in' us. If you're on our side it'll be a joy-ride. If you stick to that guy, Carshaw—"

To their ears, as to the ears of those waiting in the car at the gate, came the sound of violent blows and the wrenching open of the door. In that large house—in a room situated, too, on the side removed from the road—they could not catch Carshaw's exulting cry after a peep through the window:

"I have them! Voles and Fowle! There they are! Now you, who fought with Funston, fight for a year's pay to be earned in a minute. Here! use this wrench. You understand it. Use it on the head of any one who resists you. These scoundrels must be taken red-handed."

Voles at the first alarm sprang to his feet and whipped out a revolver. He knew that a vigorous assault was being made on the stout door. Running to the blind of the nearest window, he saw Carshaw pull out an iron bar by sheer strength and use it as a lever to pry open a sash. Tempted though he was to shoot, he dared not. There might be police outside. Murder would shatter his dreams of wealth and luxury. He must outwit his pursuers.

Rachel Craik came running from the kitchen, alarmed by the sudden hubbub.

"Fowle," he said to his amazed confederate, "stand them off for a minute or two. You, Rachel, can help. You know where to find me when the coast is clear. They cannot touch you. Remember that. They're breaking into this house without a warrant. Bluff hard, and they cannot even frame a charge against you if the girl is secured—and she will be if you give me time."

Trusting more to Rachel than to vacillating Fowle, he raced up-stairs, though his injured leg made rapid progress difficult. He ran into a room and grabbed a small bag which lay in readiness. Then he rushed toward the room in which Winifred and Mick the Wolf were listening with mixed feelings to the row which had sprung up beneath.

He tried the door. It was locked. Rachel had the key in her pocket. A trifle of that nature did not deter a man like Voles. With his shoulder he burst the lock, coming face to face with his partner in crime, who had grasped a poker in his serviceable hand.

"Atta-boy!" he yelled. "Down-stairs, and floor 'em as they come. You've one sound arm. Go for 'em—they can't lay a finger on you."

Now, it was one thing to sympathize with a helpless and gentle girl, but another to resist the call of the wild. The dominant note in Mick the Wolf was brutality, and the fighting instinct conquered even his pain. With an oath he made his way to the hall, and it needed all of Steingall's great strength to overpower him, wounded though he was.

It took Carshaw and Jim a couple of minutes to force their way in. There was a lively fight, in which the detective lent a hand. When Mick the Wolf was down, groaning and cursing because his fractured arm was broken again; when Fowle was held to the floor, with Rachel Craik, struggling and screaming, pinned beneath him by the valiant Jim, Carshaw sped to the first floor.

Soon, after using hand-cuffs on the man and woman, and leaving Jim in charge of them and Mick the Wolf, Steingall joined him. But, search as they might, they could not find either Winifred or Voles. Almost beside himself with rage, Carshaw rushed back to the grim-visaged Rachel.

"Where is she?" he cried. "What have you done with her? By Heaven, I'll kill you—"

Her face lit up with a malignant joy. "A nice thing!" she screamed. "Respectable folk to be treated in this way! What have we done, I'd like to know? Breaking into our house and assaulting us!"

"No good talking to her," said the chief. "She's a deep one—tough as they make 'em. Let's search the grounds."

CHAPTER XXIV
IN FULL CRY

Polly, the maid from the inn, waiting breathlessly intent in the car outside the gate, listened for sounds which should guide her as to the progress of events within.

Steingall left her standing on the upholstered back of the car, with her hands clutching the top of the gate. She did not descend immediately. In that position she could best hear approaching footsteps, as she could follow the running of the detective nearly all the way to the house.

Great was her surprise, therefore, to find some one unlocking the gate without receiving any preliminary warning of his advent. She was just in time to spring back into the tonneau when one-half of the ponderous door swung open and a man appeared, carrying in his arms the seemingly lifeless body of a woman.

It will be remembered that the lamps of the car spread their beams in the opposite direction. In the gloom, not only of the night but of the high wall and the trees, Polly could not distinguish features.

She thought, however, the man was a stranger. Naturally, as the rescuers had just gone toward the point whence the newcomer came, she believed that he had been directed to carry the young lady to the waiting car. Her quick sympathy was aroused.

"The poor dear!" she cried. "Oh, don't tell me those horrid people have hurt her."

Voles who had choked Winifred into insensibility with a mixture of alcohol, chloroform, and ether—a scientific anesthetic used by all surgeons, rapid in achieving its purpose and quite harmless in its effects—was far more surprised than Polly. He never expected to be greeted in this way, but rather to be met by some helper of Carshaw's posed there, and he was prepared to fight or trick his adversary as occasion demanded.

He had carried Winifred down a servants' stairs and made his way out of the house by a back door. The exit was unguarded. In this, as in many other country mansions, the drive followed a circuitous sweep, but a path through the trees led directly toward the gate. Hence, his passage had neither been observed from the hall nor overheard by Polly.

It was in precisely such a situation as that which faced him now that Voles was really superb. He was an adroit man, with ready judgment and nerves of steel.

"Not much hurt," he said quietly. "She has fainted from shock, I think."

Though he spoke so glibly, his brain was on fire with question and answer. His eyes glowered at the car and its occupant, and swept the open road on either hand.

To Polly's nostrils was wafted a strange odor, carrying reminiscences of so-called "painless" dentistry. Winifred, reviving in the open air when that hateful sponge was removed from mouth and nose, struggled spasmodically in the arms of her captor. Polly knew that women in a faint lie deathlike. That never-to-be-forgotten scent, too, caused a wave of alarm, of suspicion, to creep through her with each heart-beat.

"Where are the others?" she said, leaning over, and striving to see Voles's face.

"Just behind," he answered. "Let me place Miss Bartlett in the car."

That sounded reasonable.

"Lift her in here, poor thing," said Polly, making way for the almost inanimate form.

"No; on the front seat."

"But why? This is the best place—oh, help, *help!*"

For Voles, having placed Winifred beside the steering-pillar, seized Polly and flung her headlong onto the grass beneath the wall. In the same instant he started the car with a quick turn of the wrist, for the engine had been stopped to avoid noise, and there was no time to experiment with self-starters. He jumped in, released the brakes, applied the first speed, and was away in the direction to New York. Polly, angry and frightened, ran after him, screaming at the top of her voice.

Voles was in such a desperate hurry that he did not pay heed to his steering, and nearly ran over a motor-cyclist coming in hot haste to East Orange. The rider, a young man, pulled up and used language. He heard Polly, panting and shrieking, running toward him.

"Good gracious, Miss Barnard, what's the matter?" he cried, for Polly was pretty enough to hold many an eye.

"Is that you, Mr. Petch? Thank goodness! There's been murder done in Gateway House. That villain is carrying off the young lady he has killed. He has escaped from the police. They're in there now. Oh, catch him!"

Mr. Petch, who had dismounted, began to hop back New York-ward, while the engine emulated a machine-gun.

"It's a big car—goes fast—I'll do my best—" Polly heard him say, and he, too, was gone. She met Carshaw and the chief half-way up the drive. To them, in gasps, she told her story.

"Cool hand, Voles!" said Steingall.

"The whole thing was bungled!" cried Carshaw in a white heat. "If Clancy had been here this couldn't have happened."

Steingall took the implied taunt coolly.

"It would have been better had I followed my original plan and not helped you," he said. "You or our East Orange friend might have been killed, it is true, but Voles could not have carried the girl off so easily."

Carshaw promptly regretted his bitter comment. "I'm sorry," he said, "but you cannot realize what all this means to me, Steingall."

"I think I can. Cheer up; your car is easily recognizable. We have a cyclist known to this young lady in close pursuit. Even if he fails to catch up with Voles, he will at least give us some definite direction for a search. At present there is nothing for us to do but lodge these people in the local prison, telephone the ferries and main towns, and go back to New York. The police here will let us know what happens to the cyclist; he may even call at the Bureau. I can act best in New York."

"Do you mean now to arrest those in the house?"

"Yes, sure. That is, I'll get the New Jersey police to hold them."

"On what charge?"

"Conspiracy. At last we have clear evidence against them. Miss Polly here has actually seen Voles carrying off Miss Bartlett, who had previously been rendered insensible. If I am not mistaken in my man, Fowle will turn State's evidence when he chews on the proposition for a few hours in a cell."

"Pah—the wretch! I don't want these reptiles to be crushed; what I want is to recover Miss Bartlett. Would it not be best to leave them their liberty and watch them?"

"I've always found a seven days' remand very helpful," mused the detective.

"In ordinary crime, yes. But here we have Rachel Craik, who would suffer martyrdom rather than speak; Fowle, a mere tool, who knows nothing except what little he is told; and a thick-headed brute named Mick the Wolf, who does what his master bids him. Don't you see that in prison they are useless. At liberty they may help by trying to communicate with Voles."

"I'm half inclined to agree with you. Now to frighten them. Keep your face and tongue under control; I'll try a dodge that seldom fails."

They re-entered the house. Jim was doing sentry-go in the hall. The prisoners were sitting mute, save that Mick the Wolf uttered an occasional growl of pain; his wounded arm was hurting him sorely.

"We're not going to worry any more about you," said Steingall contemptuously as he unlocked the hand-cuffs with which he had been compelled to secure Rachel and Fowle.

"Yes, you will," was the woman's defiant cry. "Your outrageous conduct—"

"Oh, pull that stuff on some one likely to be impressed by it. It comes a trifle late in the day when Miss Winifred Marchbanks is in the hands of her friends and

Voles on his way to prison. I don't even want you, Rachel Bartlett, unless the State attorney decides that you ought to be prosecuted."

The woman's eyes gleamed like those of a spiteful cat. The detective's cool use of Winifred's right name, and of the name by which Rachel Craik herself ought to be known, was positively demoralizing. Fowle, too, was greatly alarmed. The police-officer said nothing about not wanting him. With Voles's superior will withdrawn, he began to quake again. But Rachel was a dour New Englander, of different metal to a man from the East Side.

"If you're speaking of my niece," she said, "you have been misled by the hussy, and by that man of hers there. Mr. Voles is her father. I have every proof of my words. You can bring none of yours."

Steingall, eying Fowle, laughed. "You will be able to tell us all about it in the witness-box, Rachel Bartlett," he said.

"How dare you call me by that name?"

"Because it's your right one. Craik was your mother's name. If friend Voles had only kept his hands clean, or even treated you honorably, you might now be Mrs. Ralph Meiklejohn, eh?"

He was playing with her with the affable gambols of a cat toying with a doomed mouse. Each instant Fowle was becoming more perturbed. He did not like the way in which the detective ignored him. Was he to be swallowed at a gulp when his turn came?

Even Rachel Craik was silenced by this last shot. She wrung her hands; this stern, implacable woman seemed to be on the point of bursting into tears. All the plotting and devices of years had failed her suddenly. An edifice of deception, which had lasted half a generation, had crumbled into nothingness. This man had callously exposed her secret and her shame. At that moment her heart was bitter against Voles.

The detective, skilled in the phases of criminal thought, knew exactly what was passing through the minds of both Rachel and Fowle. Revenge in the one case, safety in the other, was operating quickly, and a crisis was at hand.

But just then the angry voice of the East Orange plumber reached him: "Just imagine Petch turnin' up; him, of all men in the world! An' of course you talked nicey-nicey, an' he's such an obligin' feller that he beats it after the car! Petch, indeed!"

There was a snort of jealous fury. Polly's voice was raised in protest.

"Jim, don't be stupid. How could I tell who it was?"

"I'll back you against any girl in East Orange to find another string to your bow wherever you may happen to be," was the enraged retort.

The detective hastened to stop this lovers' quarrel, which had broken out after a whispered colloquy. He was too late. Miss Polly was on her dignity.

"Well, Mr. Petch is a real man, anyhow," came her stinging answer. "He's after them now, and he won't let them slip through his fingers like you did."

The sheer injustice of this statement rendered Jim incoherent. Petch was an old rival. When next they met, gore would flow in East Orange. But the detective's angry whisper restored the senses of both.

"Can't you two shut up?" he hissed. "Your miserable quarrel has warned our prisoners. They were on the very point of confessing everything when you blurted out that the chief rascal had escaped. I'm ashamed of you, especially after you had behaved so well."

His rebuke was merited; they were abashed into silence—too late. When he returned to the pair in the corner of the room he saw Rachel Craik's sour smile and Fowle's downcast look of calculation.

"A lost opportunity!" he muttered, but faced the situation quite pleasantly.

"You may as well remain here," he said. "I may want you, and you should realize without giving further trouble that you cannot hide from the police. Come, Mr. Carshaw, we have work before us in East Orange. Miss Winifred should be all right by this time."

Rachel Craik actually laughed. She wondered why she had lost faith in Voles for an instant.

"I'll send a doctor," went on Steingall composedly. "Your friend there needs one, I guess."

"I'd sooner have a six-shooter," roared Mick the Wolf.

"Doctors are even more deadly sometimes."

So the detective took his defeat cheerfully, and that is the worst thing a man can do—in his opponent's interests. He was rather silent as he trudged with Carshaw and the others back to the train, however.

He was asking himself what new gibe Clancy would spring on him when the story of the night's fiasco came out.

CHAPTER XXV
FLANK ATTACKS

Somewhat tired, having ridden that day to Poughkeepsie and back, Petch, nevertheless, put up a great race after the fleeing motor-car.

His muscles were rejuvenated by Polly Barnard's exciting news and no less by admiration for the girl herself. Little thinking that Jim, the plumber, was performing deeds of derring-do in the hall of Gateway House, he congratulated himself on the lucky chance which enabled him to oblige the fair Polly. He dashed into the road to Hoboken, and found, to his joy, that the dust raised by the passage of the car gave an unfailing clue to its route. Now, a well-regulated motor-cycle can run rings round any other form of automobile, no matter how many horses may be pent in the cylinders, if on an ordinary road and subjected to the exigencies of traffic.

Voles, break-neck driver though he was, dared not disregard the traffic regulations and risk a smash-up. He got the best out of the engine, but was compelled to go steadily through clusters of houses and around tree-shaded corners. To his great amazement, as he was tearing through the last habitations before crossing the New Jersey flats, he was hailed loudly from behind:

"Hi, you—pull up!"

He glanced over his shoulder. A motor-cyclist, white with dust, was riding after him with tremendous energy.

"Hola!" cried Voles, snatching another look. "What's the matter?"

Petch should have temporized, done one of a hundred things he thought of too late; but he was so breathless after the terrific sprint in which he overtook Voles that he blurted out:

"I know you—you can't escape—there's the girl herself—I see her!"

"Hell!"

Voles urged on the car by foot and finger. After him pelted Petch, with set teeth and straining eyes. The magnificent car, superb in its energies, swept through the night like the fiery dragon of song and fable, but with a speed never attained by dragon yet, else there would be room on earth for nothing save dragons. And the motor-cycle leaped and bounded close behind, stuttering its resolve to conquer the monster in front.

The pair created a great commotion as they whirred past scattered houses and emerged into the keen, cold air of the marshland. A few cars met en route actually slowed up, and heads were thrust out to peer in wonder. Women in them were scared, and enjoined drivers to be careful, while men explained laughingly that a couple of joy-riders were being chased by a motor "cop."

It was neck or nothing now for Voles, and when these alternatives offered, he never hesitated as to which should be chosen. He knew he was in desperate case.

The pace; the extraordinary appearance of a hatless man and a girl with her hair streaming wild—for Winifred's abundant tresses had soon shed all restraint of pins and twists before the tearing wind of their transit—would create a tumult in Hoboken. Something must be done. He must stop the car and shoot that pestiferous cyclist, who had sprung out of the ground as though one of Medusa's teeth had lain buried there throughout the ages, and become a panoplied warrior at a woman's cry.

He looked ahead. There was no car in sight. He peered over his shoulder. There was no cyclist! Petch had not counted on this frenzied race, and his petrol-tank was empty. He had pulled up disconsolately half a mile away, and was now borrowing a gallon of gas from an Orange-bound car, explaining excitedly that he was "after" a murderer!

Voles laughed. The fiend's luck, which seldom fails the fiend's votaries, had come to his aid in a highly critical moment. There remained Winifred. She, too, must be dealt with. Now, all who have experienced the effect of an anesthetic will understand that after the merely stupefying power of the gas has waned there follows a long period of semi-hysteria, when actual existence is dreamlike, and impressions of events are evanescent. Winifred, therefore, hardly appreciated what was taking place until the car stopped abruptly, and the stupor of cold passed almost simultaneously with the stupor of anesthesia.

But Voles had his larger plan now. With coolness and daring he might achieve it. All depended on the discretion of those left behind in Gateway House. It was impossible to keep Winifred always in durance, or to prevent her everlastingly from obtaining help. That fool of a cyclist, for instance, had he contented himself with riding quietly behind until he reached the ferry, would have wrecked the exploit beyond repair.

There remained one last move, but it was a perfect one in most ways. Would Fowle keep his mouth shut? Voles cursed Fowle in his thought. Were it not for Fowle there would have been no difficulty. Carshaw would never have met Winifred, and the girl would have been as wax in the hands of Rachel Craik. He caught hold of Winifred's arm.

"If you scream I'll choke you!" he said fiercely.

Shaken by the chloroform mixture, benumbed as the outcome of an unprotected drive, the girl was physically as well as mentally unable to resist. He coiled her hair into a knot, gagged her dexterously with a silk handkerchief—Voles knew all about gags—and tied her hands behind her back with a shoe-lace. Then he adjusted the hood and side-screens.

He did these things hurriedly, but without fumbling. He was losing precious minutes, for the telephone-wire might yet throttle him; but the periods of waiting at the ferry and while crossing the Hudson must be circumvented in some way or other. His last act before starting the car was to show Winifred the revolver he never lacked.

"See this!" he growled into her ear. "I'm not going to be held by any cop. At the least sign of a move by you to attract attention I'll put the first bullet through the cop, the second through you, and the third through myself, if I can't make my get-away. Better believe that. I mean it."

He asked for no token of understanding on her part. He was stating only the plain facts. In a word, Voles was born to be a great man, and an unhappy fate had made him a scoundrel. But fortune still befriended him. Rain fell as he drove through Hoboken. The ferry was almost deserted, and the car was wedged in between two huge mail-vans on board the boat.

Hardened rascal though he was, Voles breathed a sigh of relief as he drove unchallenged past a uniformed policeman on arriving at Christopher Street. He guessed his escape was only a matter of minutes. In reality, he was gone some ten seconds when the policeman was called to the phone. As for Petch, that valorous knight-errant crossed on the next boat, and the Hoboken police were already on the *qui vive*.

Every road into and out of New York was soon watched by sharp eyes on the lookout for a car bearing a license numbered in the tens of thousands, and tenanted by a hatless man and a girl in indoor costume. Quickly the circles lessened in concentric rings through the agencies of telephone-boxes and roundsmen.

At half past nine a patrolman found a car answering the description standing outside an up-town saloon on the East Side. Examining the register number he saw at once that blacking had been smeared over the first and last figures. Then he knew. But there was no trace of the driver. Voles and Winifred had vanished into thin air.

Mrs. Carshaw, breakfasting with a haggard and weary son, revealed that Senator Meiklejohn was at Atlantic City. He kissed her for the news.

"Meiklejohn must wait, mother," he said. "Winifred is somewhere in New York. I cannot tear myself away to Atlantic City to-day. When I have found her, I shall deal with Meiklejohn."

Then came Steingall, and he and Mrs. Carshaw exchanged a glance which the younger man missed.

Mrs. Carshaw, sitting a while in deep thought after the others had gone, rang up a railway company. Atlantic City is four hours distant from New York. By hurrying over certain inquiries she wished to make, she might catch a train at midday.

She drove to her lawyers. At her request a smart clerk was lent to her for a couple of hours. They consulted various records. The clerk made many notes on foolscap sheets in a large, round hand, and Mrs. Carshaw, seated in the train, read them many times through her gold-mounted lorgnette.

It was five o'clock when a taxi brought her to the Marlborough-Blenheim Hotel, and Senator Meiklejohn was the most astonished man on the Jersey coast at the moment when she entered unannounced, for Mrs. Carshaw had simply said to the elevator-boy: "Take me to Senator Meiklejohn's sitting-room."

Undeniably he was startled; but playing desperately for high stakes had steadied him somewhat. Perhaps the example of his stronger brother had some value, too, for he rose with sufficient affability.

"What a pleasant *rencontré*, Mrs. Carshaw," he said. "I had no notion you were within a hundred miles of the Board Walk."

"That is not surprising," she answered, sinking into a comfortable chair. "I have just arrived. Order me some sandwiches and a cup of tea. I'm famished."

He obeyed.

"I take it you have come to see me?" he said, quietly enough, though aware of a queer fluttering about the region of his heart.

"Yes. I am so worried about Rex."

"Dear me! The girl?"

"It is always a woman. How you men must loathe us in your sane moments, if you ever have any."

"I flatter myself that I am sane, yet how could I say that I loathe *your* sex, Mrs. Carshaw?"

"I wonder if your flattery will bear analysis. But there! No serious talk until I am refreshed. Do ring for some biscuits; sandwiches are apt to be slow in the cutting."

Thus by pretext she kept him from direct converse until a tea-tray, with a film of *paté de fois* coyly hidden in thin bread and butter, formed, as it were, a rampart between them.

"How did you happen on my address?" he asked smilingly.

It was the first shell of real warfare, and she answered in kind: "That was quite easy. The people at the detective bureau know it."

The words hit him like a bullet.

"The Bureau!" he cried.

"Yes. The officials there are interested in the affairs of Winifred Marchbanks."

He went ashen-gray, but essayed, nevertheless, to turn emotion into mere amazement. He was far too clever a man to pretend a blank negation. The situation was too strenuous for any species of ostrich device.

"I seem to remember that name," he said slowly, moistening his lips with his tongue.

"Of course you do. You have never forgotten it. Let us have a friendly chat about her, Senator. My son is going to marry her. That is why I am here."

She munched her sandwiches and sipped her tea. This experienced woman of the world, now boldly declared on the side of romance, was far too astute to force the man to desperation unless it was necessary. He must be given breathing-time, permitted to collect his wits. She was sure of her ground. Her case was not legally strong. Meiklejohn would discover that defect, and, indeed, it was not her object to act legally. If others could plot and scheme, she would have a finger in the pie—that was all. And behind her was the clear brain of Steingall, who had camped for days near the Senator in Atlantic City, and had advised the mother how to act for her son.

There was a long silence. She ate steadily.

"Perhaps you will be good enough to state explicitly why you are here, Mrs. Carshaw," said Meiklejohn at last.

She caught the ring of defiance in his tone. She smiled. There was to be verbal sword-play, and she was armed *cap-à-pie*.

"Just another cup of tea," she pleaded, and he wriggled uneasily in his chair. The delay was torturing him. She unrolled her big sheets of notes. He looked over at them with well-simulated indifference.

"I have an engagement—" he began, looking at his watch.

"You must put it off," she said, with sudden heat. "The most important engagement of your life is here, now, in this room, William Meiklejohn. I mentioned the detective bureau when I entered. Which do you prefer to encounter—me or an emissary of the police?"

He paled again. Evidently this society lady had claws, and would use them if annoyed.

"I do not think that I have said anything to warrant such language to me," he murmured, striving to smile deprecatingly. He succeeded but poorly.

"You sent me to drive out into the world the girl whom my son loved," was the retort. "You made a grave mistake in that. I recognized her, after a little while. I knew her mother. Now, am I to go into details?"

"I—really—I—"

"Very well. Eighteen years ago your brother, Ralph Vane Meiklejohn, murdered a man named Marchbanks, who had discovered that you and your brother were defrauding his wife of funds held by your bank as her trustees. I have here the records of the crime. I do not say that your brother, who has since been a convict and is now assisting you under the name of Ralph Voles, could be charged with that crime. Maybe 'murderer' is too strong a word for him where Marchbanks was concerned; but I do say that any clever lawyer could send you and him to the penitentiary for robbing a dead woman and her daughter, the girl whom you and he have kidnapped within the last week."

Here was a broadside with a vengeance. Meiklejohn could not have endured a keener agony were he facing a judge and jury. It was one thing to have borne this terrible secret gnawing at his vitals during long years, but it was another to find it pitilessly laid bare by a woman belonging to that very society for which he had dared so much in order to retain his footing.

He bent his head between his hands. For a few seconds thoughts of another crime danced in his surcharged brain. But Mrs. Carshaw's well-bred syllables brought him back to sanity with chill deliberateness.

"Shall I go on?" she said. "Shall I tell you of Rachel Bartlett; of the scandal to be raised about your ears, not only by this falsified trust, but by the outrageous attack on Ronald Tower?"

He raised his pallid face. He was a proud man, and resented her merciless taunts.

"Of course," he muttered, "I deny everything you have said. But, if it were true, you must have some ulterior motive in approaching me. What is it?"

"I am glad you see that. I am here to offer terms."

"Name them."

"You must place this girl, Winifred Marchbanks, under my care—where she will remain until my son marries her—and make restitution of her mother's property."

"No doubt you have a definite sum in your mind?"

"Most certainly. My lawyers tell me you ought to refund the interest as well, but Winifred may content herself with the principal. You must hand her half a million dollars!"

He sprang to his feet, livid. "Woman," he yelled, "you are crazy!"

CHAPTER XXVI
THE BITER BIT

Mrs. Carshaw focused him again through her gold-rimmed eye-glasses. "Crazy?" she questioned calmly. "Not a bit of it—merely an old woman bargaining for her son. Rex would not have done it. After thrashing you he would have left you to the law, and, were the law to step in, you would surely be ruined. I, on the other hand, do not scruple to compound a felony—that is what my lawyers call it. My extravagance and carelessness have contributed to encumber Rex's estates with a heavy mortgage. If I provide his wife with a dowry which pays off the mortgage and leaves her a nice sum as pin-money, I shall have done well."

"Half a million! I—I repudiate your statements. Even if I did not, I have no such sum at command."

"Yes, you have, or will have, which is the same thing. Shall I give you details of the Costa Rica cotton concession, arranged between you, and Jacob, and Helen Tower? They're here. As for repudiation, perhaps I have hurried matters. Permit me to go through my story at some length, quoting chapter and verse."

She spread open her papers again, after having folded them.

"Stop this wretched farce," he almost screamed, for her coolness broke up his never too powerful nervous system. "If—I agree—what guarantee is there—"

"Ah! now you're talking reasonably. I can ensure the acceptance of my terms. First, where is Winifred?"

He hesitated. Here was the very verge of the gulf. Any admission implied the truth of Mrs. Carshaw's words. She did not help him. He must take the plunge without any further impulsion. But the Senator's nerve was broken. They both knew it.

"At Gateway House, East Orange," he said sullenly. "I must tell you that my—my brother is a dare-devil. Better leave me to——"

"I am glad you have told the truth," she interrupted. "She is not at Gateway House now. Rex and a detective were there last night. There was a fight. Your brother, a resourceful scoundrel evidently, carried her off. You must find him and her. A train leaves for New York in half an hour. Come back with me and help look for her. It will count toward your regeneration."

He glanced at his watch abstractedly. He even smiled in a sickly way as he said:

"You timed your visit well."

"Yes. A woman has intuition, you know. It takes the place of brains. I shall await you in the hall. Now, don't be stupid, and think of revolvers, and poisons, and things. You will end by blessing me for my interference. Will you be ready in five minutes?"

She sat in the lounge, and soon saw some baggage descending. Then Meiklejohn joined her. She went to the office and asked for a telegraph form. The Senator had followed.

"What are you going to do?" he asked suspiciously.

"I'm wiring Rex to say that you and I are traveling to New York together, and advising him to suspend operations until we arrive. That will be helpful. You will not be tempted to act foolishly, and he will not do anything to prejudice your future actions."

He gave her a wrathful glance. Mrs. Carshaw missed no point. A man driven to desperation might be tempted to bring about an "accident" if he fancied he could save himself in that way. But, clever as a mother scheming for her son's welfare proved herself, there was one thing she could not do. Neither she nor any other human being can prevent the unexpected from happening occasionally. Sound judgment and astute planning will often gain a repute for divination; yet the prophet is decried at times. Steingall had discovered this, and Mrs. Carshaw experienced it now.

It chanced that Mick the Wolf, lying in Gateway House on a bed of pain, his injuries aggravated by the struggle with the detective, and his temper soured by Rachel Craik's ungracious ministrations, found his thoughts dwelling on the gentle girl who had forgotten her own sorrows and tended him, her enemy.

Such moments come to every man, no matter how vile he may be, and this lorn wolf was a social castaway from whom, during many years, all decent-minded people had averted their faces. His slow-moving mind was apt to be dominated by a single idea. He understood enough of the Costa Rican project to grasp the essential fact that there was money in it for all concerned, and money honestly earned, if honesty be measured by the ethics of the stock manipulator.

He realized, too, that neither Voles nor Rachel Craik could be moved by argument, and he rightly estimated Fowle as a weak-minded nonentity. So he slowly hammered out a conclusion, and, having appraised it in his narrow circle of thought, determined to put it into effect.

An East Orange doctor, who had received his instructions from the police, paid a second visit to Mick the Wolf shortly before the hour of Mrs. Carshaw's arrival in Atlantic City.

"Well, how is the arm feeling now?" he said pleasantly, when he entered the patient's bedroom.

The answer was an oath.

"That will never do," laughed the doctor. "Cheerfulness is the most important factor in healing. Ill-temper causes jerky movements and careless—"

"Oh, shucks," came the growl. "Say, listen, boss! I've been broke up twice over a slip of a girl. I've had enough of it. The whole darn thing is a mistake. I want to end it, an' I don't give a hoorah in Hades who knows. Just tell her friends that if they look for her on board the steamer *Wild Duck*, loadin' at Smith's Pier in the East River, they'll either find her or strike her trail. That's all. Now fix these bandages, for my arm's on fire."

The doctor wisely put no further questions. He dressed the wounded limb and took his departure. A policeman in plain clothes, hiding in a neighboring barn, saw him depart and hailed him: "Any news, Doc?"

"Yes," was the reply. "If my information is correct you'll not be kept there much longer."

He motored quickly to the police-station. Within the hour Carshaw, with frowning face and dreams of wreaking physical vengeance on the burly frame of Voles, was speeding across New York with Steingall in his recovered car. He simply hungered for a personal combat with the man who had inflicted such sufferings on his beloved Winifred.

The story told by Polly Barnard, and supplemented by Petch, revealed very clearly the dastardly trick practised by Voles the previous evening, while the dodge of smearing out two of the figures on the automobile's license plate explained the success attained in traversing the streets unnoticed by the police.

Steingall was inclined to theorize.

"The finding of the car puzzled me at first, I admit," he said. "Now, assuming that Mick the Wolf has not sent us off on a wild-goose chase, the locality of the steamer explains it. Voles drove all the way to the East Side, quitted the car in the neighborhood of the pier, deposited Miss Bartlett on board the vessel under some plausible pretext, and actually risked the return journey into the only part of New York where the missing auto might not be noticed at once. He's a bold rogue, and no mistake."

But Carshaw answered not. The chief glanced at him sideways, and smiled. There was a lowering fire in his companion's eyes that told its own story. Thenceforward, the run was taken in silence. But Steingall had decided on his next move. When they neared Smith's Pier Carshaw wished to drive straight there.

"Nothing of the sort," was the sharp official command. "We have failed once. Perhaps it was my fault. This time there shall be no mistakes. Turn along the next street to the right. The precinct station is three blocks down."

Somewhat surprised by Steingall's tone, the other obeyed. At the station-house a policeman, called from the men's quarters, where he was quietly reading and smoking, stated that he was on duty in the neighborhood between eight o'clock the previous evening and four o'clock that morning. He remembered seeing a car, similar to the one standing outside, pass about 9.15 P.M. It contained two people, he believed, but could not be sure, as the screens were raised owing to the rain. He did not see the car again; some drunken sailors required attention during the small hours.

The local police captain and several men in plain clothes were asked to assemble quietly on Smith's Pier. A message was sent to the river police, and a launch requisitioned to patrol near the *Wild Duck*.

Finally, Steingall, who was a born strategist, and whose long experience of cross-examining counsel rendered him wary before he took irrevocable steps in cases such as this, where a charge might fail on unforeseen grounds, made inquiries from a local ship's chandler as to the *Wild Duck*, her cargo, and her destination.

There was no secret about her. She was loading with stores for Costa Rica. The consignees were a syndicate, and both Carshaw and Steingall recognized its name as that of the venture in which Senator Meiklejohn was interested.

"Do you happen to know if there is any one on board looking after the interests of the syndicate?" asked the detective.

"Yes. A big fellow has been down here once or twice. He's going out as the manager, I guess. His name was—let me see now—"

"Voles?" suggested Steingall.

"No, that wasn't it. Oh, I've got it—Vane, it was."

Carshaw, dreadfully impatient, failed to understand all this preliminary survey; but the detective had no warrant, and ship's captains become crusty if their vessels are boarded in a peremptory manner without justification. Moreover, Steingall quite emphatically ordered Carshaw to remain on the wharf while he and others went on board.

"You want to strangle Voles, if possible," he said. "From what I've heard of him he would meet the attempt squarely, and you two might do each other serious injury. I simply refuse to permit any such thing. You have a much more pleasant task awaiting you when you meet the young lady. No one will say a word if you hug her as hard as you like."

Carshaw, agreeing to aught but delay, promised ruefully not to interfere. When the river police were at hand a nod brought several powerfully built officers closing in on the main gangway of the *Wild Duck*. The police-captain, in uniform, accompanied Steingall on board.

A deck hand hailed them and asked their business.

"I want to see the captain," said the detective.

"There he is, boss, lookin' at you from the chart-house now."

They glanced up toward a red-faced, hectoring sort of person who regarded them with evident disfavor. Some ships, loading for Central American ports at out-of-the-way wharves, do not want uniformed police on their decks.

The two climbed an iron ladder. Men at work in the forehold ceased operations and looked up at them. Their progress was followed by many interested eyes from the wharf. The captain glared angrily. He, too, had noted the presence of the stalwart contingent near the gangway, nor had he missed the police boat.

"What the—" he commenced; but the detective's stern question stopped an outburst.

"Have you a man named Voles or Vane on board?"

"Mr. Vane—yes."

"Did he bring a young woman to this ship late last night?"

"I don't see—"

"Let me explain, captain. I'm from the detective bureau. The man I am inquiring for is wanted on several charges."

The steady official tone caused the skipper to think. Here was no cringing foreigner or laborer to be brow-beaten at pleasure.

"Well, I'm—" he growled. "Here, you," roaring at a man beneath, "go aft and tell Mr. Vane he's wanted on the bridge."

The messenger vanished.

"I assume there *is* a young lady on board?" went on Steingall.

"I'm told so. I haven't seen her."

"Surely you know every one who has a right to be on the ship?"

"Guess that's so, mister, an' who has more right than the daughter of the man who puts up the dough for the trip? Strikes me you're makin' a hash of things. But here's Mr. Vane. He'll soon put you where you belong."

Advancing from the after state-rooms came Voles. He was looking at the bridge, but the police-captain was hidden momentarily by the chart-room. He gazed at Steingall with bold curiosity. He had a foot on the companion ladder when he heard a sudden commotion on the wharf. Turning, he saw Fowle, livid with terror, writhing in Carshaw's grasp.

Then Voles stood still. The shades of night were drawing in, but he had seen enough to give him pause. Perhaps, too, other less palpable shadows darkened his soul at that moment.

CHAPTER XXVII
THE SETTLEMENT

The chief disliked melodrama in official affairs. Any man, even a crook, ought to know when he is beaten, and take his punishment with a stiff upper lip. But Voles's face was white, and in one of his temperament, that was as ominous a sign as the bloodshot eyes of a wild boar. Steingall had hoped that Voles would walk quietly into the chart-room, and, seeing the folly of resistance, yield to the law without a struggle. Perhaps, under other conditions, he might have done so. It was the coming of Fowle that had complicated matters.

The strategic position was simple enough. Voles had the whole of the after-deck to himself. In the river, unknown to him, was the police launch. On the wharf, plain in view, were several policemen, whose clothes in nowise concealed their character. On the bridge, visible now, was the uniformed police-captain. Above all, there was Fowle, wriggling in Carshaw's grasp, and pointing frantically at him, Voles.

"Come right along, Mr. Vane," said Steingall encouragingly; "we'd like a word with you."

The planets must have been hostile to the Meiklejohn family in that hour. Brother William was being badly handled by Mrs. Carshaw in Atlantic City, and Brother Ralph was receiving a polite request to come up-stairs and be cuffed.

But Ralph Vane Meiklejohn faced the odds creditably. People said afterward it was a pity he was such a fire-eater. Matters might have been arranged much more smoothly. As it was, he looked back, perhaps, through a long vista of misspent years, and the glance was not encouraging. Of late, his mind had dwelt with somewhat unpleasant frequency on the finding of a dead body in the quarry near his Vermont home.

His first great crime had found him out when he was beginning to forget it. He had walked that moment from the presence of a girl whose sorrowful, frightened face reminded him of another long-buried victim of that quarry tragedy. He knew, too, that this girl had been defrauded by him and his brother of a vast sum of money, and a guilty conscience made the prospect blacker than it really was. And then, he was a man of fierce impulses, of ungovernable rage, a very tiger when his baleful passions were stirred. A wave of madness swept through him now. He saw the bright prospect of an easily-earned fortune ruthlessly replaced by a more palpable vision of prison walls and silent, whitewashed corridors. Perhaps the chair of death itself loomed through the red mist before his eyes.

Yet he retained his senses sufficiently to note the police-captain's slight signal to his men to come on board, and again he heard Steingall's voice:

"Don't make any trouble, Voles. It'll be all the worse for you in the end."

The detective's warning was not given without good cause. He knew the faces of men, and in the blazing eyes of this man he read a maniacal fury.

Voles glanced toward the river. It was nearly night. He could swim like an otter. In the sure confusion he might—Then, for the first time, he noticed the police launch. His right hand dropped to his hip.

"Ah, don't be a fool, Voles!" came the cry from the bridge. "You're only making matters worse."

A bitter smile creased the lips of the man who felt the world slipping away beneath him. His hand was thrust forward, not toward the occupants of the bridge, but toward the wharf. Fowle saw him and yelled. A report and the yell merged into a scream of agony. Voles was sure that Fowle had betrayed him, and took vengeance. There was a deadly certainty in his aim.

Steingall, utterly fearless when action was called for, swung himself down by the railings. He was too late. A second report, and Voles crumpled up.

His bold spirit had not yielded nor his hand failed him in the last moment of his need. A bullet was lodged in his brain. He was dead ere the huge body thudded on the deck.

When Carshaw found Winifred in a cabin—to open the door they had to obtain the key from Voles's pocket—the girl was sobbing pitifully. She heard the revolver shots, and knew not what they betokened. She was so utterly shaken by these last dreadful hours that she could only cling to her lover and cry in a frightened way that went to his heart:

"Oh, take me away, Rex! It was all my fault. Why did I not trust you? Please, take me away!"

He fondled her hair and endeavored to kiss the tears from her eyes.

"Don't cry, little one!" he whispered. "All your troubles have ended now."

It was a simple formula, but effective. When repeated often enough, with sufficiently convincing caresses, she became calmer. When he brought her on deck all signs of the terrible scene enacted there had been removed. She asked what had caused the firing, and he told her that Voles was arrested. It was sufficient. So sensitive was she that the mere sound of the dead bully's name made her tremble.

"I remember now," she whispered. "I was sure he had killed you. I knew you would follow me, Rex. When I saw you I forgot all else in the joy of it. Are you sure you are not injured?"

At another time he would have laughed, but her worn condition demanded the utmost forbearance.

"No, dearest," he assured her. "He did not even try to hurt me. Now let me take you to my mother."

The captain, thoroughly scared by the events he had witnessed, came forward with profuse apologies and offers of the ship's hospitality. Carshaw felt that the man was not to blame, but the *Wild Duck* held no attractions for him. He hurried Winifred ashore.

Steingall came with them. The district police would make the official inquiries as a preliminary to the inquest which would be held next day. Carshaw must attend, but Winifred would probably be excused by the authorities. He conveyed this information in scraps of innuendo. Winifred did not know of Voles's death or the shooting of Fowle till many days had passed.

Fowle did not die. He recovered, after an operation and some months in a hospital. Then Carshaw befriended him, obtained a situation for him, and gave him money to start life in an honest way once more.

There was another scene when Mrs. Carshaw brought Meiklejohn to her apartment and found Rex and Winifred awaiting them. Winifred, of course, had never seen the Senator, and there was nothing terrifying to her in the sight of a haggard, weary-looking, elderly gentleman. She was far more fluttered by meeting Rex's mother, who figured in her mind as a domineering, cruel, old lady, elegantly merciless, and gifted with a certain skill in torture by words.

Mrs. Carshaw began to dispel that impression promptly.

"My poor child!" she cried, with a break in her voice, "what you have undergone! Can you ever forgive me?"

Carshaw, ignoring Meiklejohn, whispered to his mother that Winifred should be sent to bed. She was utterly worn out. One of the maids should sleep in her room in case she awoke in fright during the night.

When left alone with Meiklejohn he intended to scarify the man's soul. But he was disarmed at the outset. The Senator's spirit was broken. He admitted everything; said nought in palliation. He could have taken no better line. When Mrs. Carshaw hastened back, fearing lest her plans might be upset, she found her son giving Winifred's chief persecutor a stiff dose of brandy.

The tragedy of Smith's Pier was allowed to sink into the obscurity of an ordinary occurrence. Fowle's unhappily-timed appearance was explained by Rachel Craik when her frenzy at the news of Voles's death had subsided.

A chuckling remark by Mick the Wolf that "There'd been a darned sight too much fuss about that slip of a girl, an' he had fixed it," alarmed her.

She sent Fowle at top speed to Smith's Pier to warn Voles. He arrived in time to be shot for his pains.

Carshaw and Winifred were married quietly. Their honeymoon consisted of the trip to Massachusetts when he began work in the cotton mill. Meiklejohn fulfilled his promise. When the Costa Rica cotton concession reached its zenith he sold out, resigned his seat in the Senate and transferred to Winifred railway cash and gilt-edged bonds to the total value of a half a million dollars. So the young bride enriched her husband, but Carshaw refused to desert his business. He will die a millionaire, but he hopes to live like one for a long time.

Petch and Jim fought over Polly. There was talk about it in East Orange, and Polly threw both over; the latest gossip is that she is going to marry a police-inspector.

Mrs. Carshaw, Sr., still visits her "dear friend," Helen Tower. Both of them speak highly of Meiklejohn, who lives in strict seclusion. He is very wealthy; since he ceased to strive for gold it has poured in on him.

Winifred secured an allowance for Rachel Craik sufficient to live on, and Mick the Wolf, whose arm was never really sound again, was given a job on the Long Island estate as a watcher.

Quite recently, when the young couple came in to New York for a week-end's shopping—rendered necessary by the establishment of day and night nurseries—they entertained Steingall and Clancy at dinner in the Biltmore. Naturally, at one stage of a pleasant meal, the talk turned on those eventful months, October and November, 1913. As usual, Clancy waxed sarcastic at his chief's expense.

"He's as vain as a star actor in the movies," he cackled. "Hogs all the camera stuff. Wouldn't give me even a flash when the big scene was put on."

Steingall pointed a fat cigar at him.

"Do you know what happened to a frog when he tried to emulate a bull?" he said.

"I know what happened to a bull one night in East Orange," came the ready retort.

"The solitary slip in an otherwise unblemished career," sighed the chief. "Make the most of it, little man. If I allowed myself to dwell on your many blunders I'd lie down and die."

Winifred never really understood these two. She thought their bickering was genuine.

"Why," she cried, "you are wonderful, both of you! From the very beginning you peered into the souls of those evil men. You, Mr. Clancy, seemed to sense a great mystery the moment you heard Rachel Craik speak to the Senator outside the club that night. As for you, Mr. Steingall, do you know what the lawyers told Rex and me soon after our marriage?"

"No, ma'am," said Steingall.

"They said that if you hadn't sent Rex's mother to Atlantic City we might never have recovered a cent of the stolen money. Sheer bluff, they called it. We would have had the greatest difficulty in establishing a legal case."

Steingall weighed the point for a moment.

"Sometimes I'm inclined to think that the police know more about human nature than any other set of men," he said, at last, evidently choosing his words with care. "Perhaps I might except doctors. They, too, see us as we are. But the dry legal mind does not allow sufficiently for what is called in every-day speech a guilty conscience. In this case these people knew they had done you and your father and mother a great wrong, and that knowledge was never absent from their thoughts. It colored every word they uttered, governed every action. That's a heavy handicap, ma'am. It's the deciding factor in the never-ending struggle between the police and the criminal classes. The most callous crook walking Broadway in freedom to-night—a man who would scoff at the notion that he is bothered by any conscience at all—never passes a policeman without an instinctive sense of danger. And that is what beats him in the long run. Crime may be a form of lunacy—indeed, I look on it in that light myself—but, luckily for mankind, crime cannot stifle conscience."

The chief's tone had become serious; he appeared to awake to its gravity when he found the young wife's eyes fixed on his with a certain awe. He broke off the lecture suddenly.

"Why," he cried, smiling broadly, and jerking the cigar toward Clancy, "why, ma'am, if we cops hadn't some sort of a pull, what chance would a shrimp like him have against any one of real intelligence?"

"That's what he regards as handing me a lemon for my Orange," grinned Clancy.

Winifred laughed. The curtain can drop on the last act of her adventures to the mirthful music of her happiness.

THE END

Lector House believes that a society develops through a two-fold approach of continuous learning and adaptation, which is derived from the study of classic literary works spread across the historic timeline of literature records. Therefore, we aim at reviving, repairing and redeveloping all those inaccessible or damaged but historically as well as culturally important literature across subjects so that the future generations may have an opportunity to study and learn from past works to embark upon a journey of creating a better future.

This book is a result of an effort made by Lector House towards making a contribution to the preservation and repair of original ancient works which might hold historical significance to the approach of continuous learning across subjects.

HAPPY READING & LEARNING!

LECTOR HOUSE LLP
E-MAIL: lectorpublishing@gmail.com

9 789353 441098

Ingram Content Group UK Ltd.
Milton Keynes UK
UKHW011824170323
418736UK00003B/206